westland ltd
MANSURI, MACABRE

Sudhir Thapliyal was born and schooled in Mussoorie to where he has returned. A graduate of the University of Allahabad, he did his Masters in Business Administration (MBA) from the Indian Institute of Management (IIM), Calcutta.

He was a senior journalist with *The Statesman* and today is a freelance journalist, writer and documentary filmmaker. He was nominated for the Rhodes Scholarship in 1967 and is a 1972 Fellow of the World Press Institute, St Paul, Minn. (USA).

Many of his short stories and features have been published in leading magazines and newspapers. He has written the screenplay of a telefilm based on Ruskin Bond's novel *Room on the Roof.* He is currently working on a screenplay for a Bollywood producer.

His published books include *Hello! Mister Tee* (Srishti Publications), renamed *The Loves and Life of Mike Tarrance* (Genesis Publishing, a division of A.H. Wheeler), *War at Lambidhar* (Genesis Publishing) and *Crossing the Road* (Roli Books).

Mansuri, Macabre

SUDHIR THAPLIYAL

Westland Ltd

westland ltd
61, 2nd Floor, Silverline Building, Alapakkam Main Road, Maduravoyal, Chennai 600095
93, 1st floor, Sham Lal Road, Daryaganj, New Delhi 110002

First published by westland ltd 2010

Copyright © Sudhir Thapliyal 2010

10 9 8 7 6 5 4 3 2 1

ISBN: 9789380658537

This is a work of fiction. Names, characters, places and incidents are either the product of the author's imagination or are used fictitiously and any resemblance to any actual person, living or dead, events or locales is entirely coincidental.

Typeset in Cambria by SÜRYA, New Delhi

For
Dr Nisha Thapliyal, Ph.D, and
legal eagle, Tushna

ACKNOWLEDGEMENTS

Ruchi and Neelam, Namita and Akhi, Anu and Rajiv, Adarsh Puri, Raku Jayal, Swati and Nikhil, Shivan, Lekha and Saurabh, Sandy and Mother (Archana), doctors and nurses at the North Point, and all those who called on me in my long moments of supine repose, many thanks. My sisters, Guddi and Rachu, my friends Bunny and Jug, much gratitude.

*If you eliminate all logical solutions to a problem,
the illogical is probably true.*

—Sherlock Holmes

PROLOGUE

Why? Why is it that we find the mask of death repulsive? Even frightening. Specially, when only a few hours ago the face was a smiling, radiantly happy complexity of muscle and nerves. It had led me, and others, to believe that all was well with them and the kingdom of whichever God they were living in at that moment.

But now rigor mortis had set in and everything was frozen in eternity like some early daguerreotype. What they call the smile of death.

Is life a tragedy or a comedy? Or is death vice versa? Or as the wondering man asks the sage: what is the meaning and purpose of being born? And when the sage tells him that it is only to sleep, eat and defaecate, the man gives him a derisive look and loses all faith in the sage's wisdom. Till such time when he gives deeper thought to what the sage had said and the ramifications of that line of thought. And then he says that was truly sage-like.

Two lonely, superstitious, naïve and God-fearing women lived, in the recent past, in a small hill town. The townspeople referred to them as The Sisters though they had proper names. The label stuck to them as it does to the blind, the deaf and dumb and the lame.

One day they were murdered. The time, day and date do not matter to the dead. They become a headache only for those who have to live with the depressing fact.

This, then, is a narration of a heinous crime. The need to tell this story is born out of the grim fact that it can also happen to some of us. It has been gleaned from accounts kept by some of the participants, court documents, eyewitness reports, speculation and hearsay. Some of the facts may or may not be true.

Even then it is a guide, a signpost for the cleverer traveller as he or she wends their way along the twisting, turning and tortuous path that we call life. It is a good idea to make a note of it. Whether the message will be heeded or not is again in the realm of the inscrutable.

The writer is fully aware that many people will see similarities in their lives with the characters in this novel. However, none is intended. But they may also have been victims of the same mix of mysticism and ignorance coupled with naivety, superstition and gullibility that mark the lives of millions of people worldwide.

This then is in essence the story of The Sisters who become victims of their own ignorance, naivety and insecurity that, in turn, were fully exploited by a ruthless, egomaniacal psychopath determined to inflict his will and his drug-induced ideas on human mortality.

But as the saying goes: what is the point of killing someone hellbent on suicide? Is there a point at all? Maybe, then maybe not, as someone I know often says when confronted with such a simple question. And he chucks you under the chin after saying that. After all, life and death are just two sides of the same coin, the man has often remarked.

And it is also said that such and such man or woman's life was a lie. But no man's or for that matter woman's life can be a very bad lie. At its worst it is nine-tenths true for as long as it continues at all.

⸺⟨●●●⟩⸺

ONE

A nagging drizzle bothered me because it leaked through the hole in my umbrella. An industrious and enterprising rat had chewed out a neat hole where it really mattered. I walked up to Cliff Hall, the collar of my raincoat turned up, but it was doing no good because a steady stream of water kept drilling its way through the hole and down the narrow of my back.

My friend Mantri's wife, Rajni, had for the first

time in her life, rung up on the morning after my sixty-second birthday to ask me if I had read the morning paper.

'If you haven't, better brace yourself for bad news . . . the sisters have been murdered,' she had said in one breath.

I said, what? And stupidly asked, why? She said she didn't know. Hung over as I was with too much drink the night before to celebrate another birthday, it took me time to clear the cobwebs that seemed to be clogging my mind. All she said was that I'd better come up to Cliff Hall.

And that was why I was braving the cold and the rain as I trudged up the hill. In my neck of the woods the newspaper doesn't arrive till noon.

For a moment I stood at the old ramshackle gate that seemed to be held together by wires and which was rarely opened to strangers. But that morning it was wide open with a motley group of press and police collected around on the main road. Inside, a team of detectives was going about its business. The station officer, who knew me, saw me and waved me in.

I walked in. Just to be poetic—because that was the mood there on that rain-soaked morning—I imagined myself, rather pompously, walking through the 'portals to the abode of the dead'. When, in the cold light of reality, I only walked through that crazily hanging gate into what was once the house of two living, smiling and beautiful human beings.

TWO

Cliff Hall was where the sisters lived in the hill town of Mansuri. It was the kind of town that had in its two-hundred-year-old history been home to all kinds of rich men, poor men, saints and thugs; refugees from all over the world including kings, shopkeepers, writers, artists and the Dalai Lama. I am one of those writers. And to me has fallen the task of documenting the events that preceded and followed the murder of two women.

The sisters had been there for a long time. Some said from 1947 but I knew they had moved there in the mid-Fifties when their father bought the property from a nawab.

Earlier, they had lived in an abandoned house called Noor Manzil. Another Muslim gentleman, in the stormy and violent days before the official Partition, had left it to its fate. This house was later acquired on an 'as is where is' basis because the Muslim gentleman farmer had decided to go back to what was his ancestral home and lands in the Punjab—West Punjab, that is—in the emerging State of Pakistan.

The sisters, then little girls, and their refugee family moved into the house effortlessly in those troubled and disjointed times. No questions were asked because there was nobody to ask them. The house came to be called Sirdar Villa because the Sirdars from Sialkot (now in Pakistan) lived there. And there were, at that time, quite a few of them. The gentleman farmer was forgotten and so was Noor Manzil. It was the new India.

The sisters went to the convent school on top of the hill and, like other girls in the Fifties, prepared for a middle-class existence. They learnt all the niceties of demeanour, posture and such frivolous but nevertheless necessary baggage for a well-settled married life. Alongside they picked up skills like knitting, needlework and crochet. They painted in desultory fashion, nothing original or daring.

Their art work was standard—still-lifes of flowers and sunrises and sunsets. The sun setting behind mountains and the sun rising out of the sea, which of course they had never seen. You see, the sea is miles away from the mountains of the subcontinent. Like the other girls they did portraits of each other, some of them very flattering to the subject. Along the way they learnt about the bees and the birds and some of them dared to read steamy romances away from the ever-watchful eyes of the nuns. All in all, they were moulded into well-behaved little women by the time they finished school.

Some of their class wanted to study further and joined colleges in Delhi. Only one of them wanted to be a doctor. Kamlesh, the elder sister, went to France to become a garment designer. Her mother and father saw nothing wrong with that and unlike a majority of Indian parents went along with her plans. As her father fondly said, 'Kamlesh is my eldest son.' And so Kamlesh found herself in Paris where her schoolgirl French was just about good enough to get by.

She was a curiosity. An exotic member of the species. She wisely chose to wear Indian clothes and rarely put on a skirt and a blouse. That was a smart move because she established her identity and her personality early on. Besides, like most Indian women, she wasn't leggy enough to carry off a skirt. The other girls training with her were rather frivolous, wore makeup and had boyfriends.

Kamlesh was a serious student, and she applied herself to her work with total dedication. Her teachers were impressed and encouraged her, and soon she was turning out work that caught the eye of Paris' leading design house, Chanel. It was Coco Chanel herself who thought Kamlesh had something special and commissioned her to design a line highlighting Eastern, particularly Indian, formal wear.

Things would have gone on and on in that fairytale world of Paris high fashion but for an incident that forced Kamlesh to return to India and Mansuri. She was shaping up into a top-class designer and the fashion world knew about her talent. A bright future lay ahead but a cable from home put an end to that.

It simply said: PAPPI IN LOVE WITH KUKKU stop MATTER SERIOUS stop COME HOME stop PAPAJI stop

Papaji was her doting father. He was seemingly a simple, religious-minded Sikh who owned a small shop that sold handmade woollen garments which were very popular with tourists in the hill resort. It was a small business that did well despite the cheap machine-made woollens that were flooding the market from Ludhiana. He had maintained his specialisation with the help of a small army of women workers who knitted pullovers, cardigans, shawls, scarves, babies' frocks and booties and so on. They were copies from knitting books and fashion plates in English magazines. It was his idea that Kamlesh go to Paris and learn more about design and colour so that their products would have a European look now that imports were banned.

Pappi was Kamlesh's younger sister. In the years that Kamlesh had been away in Paris, Pappi had grown up to be a beautiful woman with an hourglass figure, skin like glazed porcelain and gazelle-like eyes. She was more in the tradition of Persian princesses and there was every chance one of her ancestors had been from that exotic country. Besides being strikingly beautiful, she was an intelligent girl, spoke well in the convent tradition and was easily the pick of girls on display in the Sikh community of Mansuri.

Kukku was her cousin. A tall and elegant man, handsome in a central Asian way and without doubt the most attractive man in the community. He too ran a clothes shop located in the same bazaar. But he was in a bigger league. He sold readymade garments, employed several salesmen to sell his products and had saved enough money to buy himself a house separate from the rest of his family. In the years after Partition, he too had grown up in the ménage that was Sirdar Villa. He was older than Pappi and about the same age as Kamlesh. In a manner of speaking they had known each other right from the days they were children. They mixed easily because they were cousins but no one had foreseen them falling in love with each other. Perhaps, even the two of them didn't know that one day their camaraderie would turn into love and lead to the consequent heartbreak.

The Air-India flight that brought Kamlesh back to India was met by her mother, father and her sister Pappi. They had a tearful reunion as at it had been nearly five years that Kamlesh had been abroad. For her, time had flown by and it only seemed like yesterday, but for the others it had been a long separation.

The questions came in a rush and Kamlesh was hard put to answer all three of them simultaneously. Pappi was the most excited of all of them, and now that she had discarded her pigtails and frocks for a stylish hairdo on the lines of the reigning star of the Bombay film world, and in a form-hugging salwar kameez, she looked a beautiful woman in her prime. For Kamlesh it was going to take time to come to terms with the fact that Pappi was no longer the young girl who trailed her around like a puppy, ready to fetch and carry anything for her elder sister whom she adored.

Most of the talk revolved around how beautiful Paris was and how much Kamlesh was missing it already. What Pappi did not know was that her sister had been summoned home because of her involvement with Kukku. She also did not know that there had been a family plan to marry Kukku and Kamlesh.

In a rather insignificant ceremony many years ago, the parents of Kamlesh and Kukku had informally agreed to marry the two of them when they had finished their studies. That was the way things were done. While cousins as a rule did not marry each other, the rule was more flexible among the Sikhs in Muslim-dominated Sialkot, where it was difficult to find a boy in their clan who was not an immediate relative.

However, times had changed and both Kamlesh and Kukku had grown up to be independent-thinking types and more 'modern' than their parents. This was a result of the breakdown of the system their parents had known before Partition.

In pre-Partition days parents had the quaint notion that their offspring would listen to them in matters of the heart without a murmur. Of course, there were always those who eloped. Punjabi history and mythology were full of such romances. But times had indeed changed and in rather dramatic circumstances. India was a new world and the new world had new norms. It was all very well to have nostalgic memories of the good old days. But the harsh reality of surviving in what was palpably an alien territory was different.

Kamlesh, and more so, Pappi, could not relate to the world of Sialkot though they were born there and brought to Mansuri as little girls. They had little or no memories of that part of their childhood. They often heard of Aunty Gul and Uncle Dilshad but these were just names of friends of their parents who had stayed behind because they were Muslims. The only distinct memories of their childhood rested on friends they'd made in school and in Sialkot.

Even the Sirdar clan had broken up after ten years, as they found independent housing and shops in Mansuri. They met, of course, but for the young it was a mere formality. It was more fun with their new friends with whom they went roller-skating and for picnics to many of the beautiful hill town's waterfalls and streams. Films from Hollywood, like *Roman Holiday* and the *Sound of Music* were more to their taste.

~

It was a long drive from New Delhi to Mansuri. The asthmatic pre-war Chevrolet taxi finally deposited the reunited family at the taxi stand in the hill town and they got off and heaved a sigh of relief. Their driver, another Sikh, who like them had made it safely to India after the Partition, thanked the Gurus for having brought them home safely. And in one piece. For it was a hazardous trip, what with bandits on the roads and the last treacherous leg up the narrow mountain road that curved around hairpin bends on its way up the hill. Many a car and bus had gone over the edge of the road and the town people rarely ventured into the plains. So much so that many of them had not even seen a train, though the rail head wasn't more than an hour's drive away.

THREE

The family conclave began in the congested drawing room filled with all kinds of furniture which should have been thrown out fifty years ago. The walls were adorned with pictures of Queen Elizabeth II and other British monarchs and their sundry relatives even ten years after Independence.

'Pappi wants to get married,' Papaji said in his soft voice.

'To Kukku,' Mummyji added and arched her eyebrows.

Kamlesh looked bemusedly at the three of them and said, 'Well?'

'But we won't allow it,' Mummyji said.

'And why not?' Kamlesh asked.

'Beta, you must understand. Cousins do not marry cousins. Times have changed. Our circumstances today are different,' Papaji said. 'It is a question of izzat.'

'But you two married and you are cousins,' Pappi interjected and added, 'What is this sudden izzat-vizzat business?'

'That was in Sialkot. We are now in India. There are plenty of Sikh boys easily available. And Kukku has cut off his hair and beard and become a *mona*. He can't be called a Sikh anymore,' Mummyji said.

'But I don't want to marry any Sikh boy,' Pappi said.

'Beta,' chimed in Papaji. 'We will get you a boy you like. A boy educated like you and from a good family. I have already received several proposals for you. And every one sounds better than the other,' Papaji said in his apparently mild manner.

'Pappi, you don't have to marry if you don't want to,' Kamlesh said.

'Hai! She must marry. She can't stay a spinster,' Mummyji remonstrated.

'Well, if I can't marry Kukku then I don't want to

marry,' Pappi said petulantly and ran off sobbing to her bedroom.

The three of them looked at each other. No one spoke. Kamlesh got up and went to the kitchen and put a kettle to boil on the electric heater. She brewed some tea, heated the milk and put it all together on a tray and carried it back to the drawing room. They sipped their tea in silence. After a while Mummyji got up and went off to the kitchen to prepare the evening meal.

Papaji paced around and then began to fiddle with the big radio in the corner of the room. He got a channel in Urdu and sat down on a sofa to listen to what the news reader was saying. In between the static the man's voice on the radio droned on. Kamlesh could make out a few words and the prominent words were '*jung*' and 'Chinese'. She asked her father what the news was and the old man hushed her as he sat listening to the broadcast. She had not heard Urdu being spoken in many years and her knowledge of it was rudimentary. So, she didn't know that the Chinese had invaded India.

That night Pappi ran away from home and straight into the arms of Kukku. The young man, shocked by her audacity, pleaded with her to go back to her father's house. She told him rather melodramatically that she'd rather die than go back to that old fossil. They wrestled with the problem the whole night but by morning Kukku knew he was getting into a very dicey situation. His rather strong-headed woman wasn't all sugar and spice. She had a twist to her personality he realised he may not be able to cope with. As the sun rose he heard Pappaji's voice. The old man was at his doorstep and he had no choice but to let him in.

'Kukku,' the old man shouted. 'Open up or I'll break the door down.'

Kukku opened the door to see the old man holding a Webly and Scott .32-bore revolver which he was pointing rather steadily at his balls.

'Where is the bitch?' he roared.

Kukku had always known him to be a mild-mannered man. This was another side to Papaji's personality that he was seeing. Completely taken aback, he waved in the direction of his sitting room where Pappi sat defiantly, her chin held high and her eyes blazing with anger.

Her father walked up to her and with surprising strength grabbed her by her long and lustrous hair and dragged her out of the house. She screamed in pain and abused him in English. But he didn't let go and smacked her with the butt of his revolver. The shock of being hit and that too by her usually gentle Papaji, silenced Pappi. He dragged her through the deserted streets to Cliff Hall where he took her to her room and ordered her to cut off her hair. When she hesitated he handed her a pair of large scissors used to cut cloth with and said he would do it himself if she didn't. Cowered and in obvious pain, the girl did what he said. She hacked away at her beautiful locks of which she had been inordinately proud. The old man gathered her fallen hair, took it outside to the lawn and set it on fire.

He had done it before. Back in the days of Partition, Hindus and Muslims had attacked each other on trains carrying refugees to and fro—India to Pakistan and vice versa. He had told his young sisters-in-law, who were great beauties, that if their train was stopped by any mob, they should shoot themselves with the revolvers he had given them rather than get raped. Before that he had shorn off their beautiful manes, dirtied their faces with coal dust and made them wear their servants' cheap clothes. The sisters were tiny tots then, but they remembered what their father had done to their aunts.

In many ways, the winter that followed was a bitter one. The country as a whole was reeling under the shock of having taken a beating on its northern borders. The Prime Minister was deeply hurt at the betrayal by the Chinese—people he considered his countrymen's brothers. In Cliff Hall the arguments for and against Pappi's marriage to Kukku continued at various degrees of heat. At any rate, Pappi had been forbidden to step out of the house unescorted and there was no way she was allowed to talk to Kukku. The man in question had left for the warmer climate of the plains and when last heard from was holidaying with cousins in Bombay.

Pappi languished, looking vacantly out of the bay window in her room and watched the depressing gloomy days of winter pass her by. Kamlesh baked a cake for her but she refused to eat and was on what could be best described as a hunger strike. She had become wan and thin and the spring had gone out of her step. She prowled around her room and the family sitting outside in the drawing room heard her slipper shod feet slither across the carpet in a dull, monotonous rhythm.

After a few weeks everyone had quite got used to the way things were. Mummyji went about with her household chores, Papaji made his regular visits to the gurdwara. The shop had been closed for the winter. Kamlesh knitted. Her efforts from time to time to cheer up Pappi were like banging her head against a stone wall. The only change was that Pappi would eat some biscuits with her tea but she was still avoiding food of any kind. Outside, snow draped the hills like a starchy white sheet and the water pipes were frozen and in many places they had burst. Electricity came and went and Papaji's sole entertainment was severely affected as the radio would come and go with the power.

Most times all of them sat huddled around a Canadian stove and rarely was a word exchanged. If at all, it would be Mummyji exhorting them to eat something or the other. Kamlesh sat with her knitting or wrote long letters to her friends in Paris. Posting those letters gave her the excuse to walk to the post office and that was the only physical activity she indulged in. She would walk in the ankle-deep snow that was fast becoming a muddy slush—a lonely figure draped from head to toe in a black shawl looking neither left nor right. She made two mandatory stops. One was at the Lala's shop where she bought roasted peanuts. The next was near the post office where a newspaper hawker sat huddled in a corner regardless of the weather. Kamlesh, possibly out of a sense of charity because she only glanced at the headlines, bought a paper or a magazine. It was a dreary and depressing lifestyle but they all seemed to be quite satisfied with it.

⸺⁖⁖⁖⸺

FOUR

To an outside and impartial observer like Dr Jadu Ram Mishra, the town's homeopath, the situation in the household at Cliff Hall was definitely abnormal. As he told his friend Satya Prasad Kala, the headmaster of the local government school, 'Kala Sahab things are rather topsy-turvy. The other day I had gone there to look at the younger girl. She had fever and I was told she had not eaten any solid food for weeks. When I asked why, they all shrugged their shoulders like it wasn't a matter of great concern. I examined the patient and found she was highly malnourished, depressed to the point of listlessness and unable to answer my simple questions. She was close to bald and looked like a Buddhist nun. All the father said was that it was the will of God.'

Kala Sahab had known the family from the day they had come to Mussoorie, in 1946. In fact he had given tuitions to the girls. So, one could say he knew them quite well. An outspoken and honest man to a fault, he sniffily dismissed the good doctor's report by saying, 'God, my foot. It is their damned father. He is an obstinate ass, if there ever was one. And the mother. Well, let's just say the less said about her the better. Anyway, what did you prescribe?'

The two men had been walking along the Mall as was their wont in all weathers. The sun had been struggling to make a comeback and a faint light reflected off the snow, giving it a ghostly glow. Snow melted from rooftops and from time to time some tree or the other dusted off its white mantle. With a loud whoosh a large chunk of frozen snow would come hurtling to the ground and crash, and fine snow would powder the ground around it.

'I prescribed some medicine for her cold but I told them what she needed was to eat regularly. And, of course, some exercise. I tell you, nothing like a brisk walk to keep you well,' Dr Mishra said.

'More than a brisk walk, what people in that house need is a breath of fresh air. I mean, they have to open the windows of their minds and face the times. The old Sirdar and his Sirdarni live in a non-existent world. First, they send the children to study in a convent run by Italian nuns with a different view of building character. By the time the children grow up, they have developed minds of their own and, nourished by a first-class, modern education, want to step out of the medieval world of their parents. And then, the doors are slammed in their faces and they become virtual prisoners of their parents' mindset. It is a terrible state of affairs,' Kala Sahab observed.

'What's all that supposed to mean?' the doctor asked.

'Look, the whole town knows that the younger girl, Pappi, and Sirdar Kulwant Singh's son Kukku, are in love. They want to marry but the girl's mother and father are dead set against it. That in a nutshell is the story. The girl has gone into depression and that explains her behaviour,' Kala Sahab said.

'Well, the two lovers could run off, couldn't they?' the doctor suggested.

'Yes, they could—but they won't. The parents have cast an insidious spell on the girl. Looking at them you can't guess it. On the surface, everything seems normal. The father, with his worry beads and long white beard, looks like a Biblical patriarch. A man who can do no wrong in the eyes of God and man. That's humbug. And the mother—with her head covered at all times, eyes downcast as she walks on the road, and her voice a murmur as she talks to acquaintances, is a female Jekyll-and-Hyde,' Headmaster Kala explained.

'What is Jekyll and Hyde?' the doctor asked, confused.

'*Who* are Jekyll and Hyde,' Kala Sahab corrected him. 'They make up a fictional character created by the great English writer Robert Louis Stevenson. It is a story of opposing natures—what you doctors call a split personality. He was, willy-nilly, both good and evil—till such time as he discovered a panacea which got rid of his evil side,' Kala said in the best manner of a pedagogue.

'Hmm,' said the doctor, and asked Kala what he meant by the father being a bit of a fraud.

'Look, you couldn't come over from Pakistan in those days with an unscarred mind. Their journey was fraught with all kinds of horrors. Don't forget that there were Muslims looting, raping and killing Hindus and Sikhs, and the Hindus and Sikhs were doing the same thing to the Muslims. I know for a fact that this kind-looking gentleman actually killed a few people who got in his and his family's way. He is a tough-minded one, despite his mild appearance,' Kala explained.

The doctor chewed on that bit of information.

They were approaching the end of their walk and, with the usual goodbyes, promised to meet the next day at the same time. The two of them had become a fixture on the Mall. The doctor was a fastidious man and the teacher very upright and proper. You could say they were friends, in a manner of speaking. However, it is doubtful if they viewed their relationship in such strong terms. They would probably say they were well acquainted with each other. At any rate, they were from opposite ends of the ideological spectrum. The doctor was a fundamentalist Hindu. The pedagogue was a liberal. And the 'twain could never entirely meet.

FIVE

Winter moved on to spring. By March there were sunny days punctuated by stormy ones. A general awakening could be discerned all around as the fruit trees flowered, swallows and swifts began to dart in and out of their nests, and the Siberian geese flew north. The schools began their new terms in earnest. Up at the convent on the hill, children's voices could be heard once again after a dull silence of three months. Shouts of 'Children, come here' or 'Children, don't go there' could be heard from time to time as the nuns and teachers hustled their charges from classroom to dining room or to their dormitories.

Miss Lewis presided over her class as she had been doing for the last forty years. Hundreds of girls had passed under her nose and she remembered all of them with great fondness. She was undoubtedly a good teacher. Some even said she was a great teacher. What no one doubted was her affection and good nature. Former students on visits to Mansuri would make it a point to call on her and there were many who only came back to Mansuri so as to spend time with her. Importantly, she was a great sounding board and the girls, now mature women, married and with children, and mostly unsatisfactory husbands, confided in her their joys and sorrows. For most of them marriage had become a mindless existence. Their lives revolved around children who were mostly away at school, getting on somehow with in-laws, and husbands that they only saw at night.

Kamlesh had mentally tortured herself through the winter trying to resolve the problem at home, and she desperately needed someone to talk to. She thought of Miss Lewis and one day, walked up the hill to the convent where she met Miss Lewis after school hours. The old teacher lived in a small cottage on the fringes of the convent. It was a functional little house and Miss Lewis had put on a kettle to make her evening tea.

When Kamlesh knocked at her door she was pleasantly surprised and after a hug and a kiss made Kamlesh sit in the most comfortable chair in the cottage.

'How have you been, my child?' she asked.

'I've been all right, Miss Lewis,' Kamlesh answered.

'And how was life in Paris? Is it really all as beautiful as it is in postcards? Oh, and talking of postcards, many thanks for the ones you sent me from time to time. I've kept them all. See, I'll show you,' she said.

Miss Lewis rose from the straightbacked chair she had been sitting on next to a small table that served as her work desk. It was piled high with students' answer books waiting to be checked. Miss Lewis had aged gracefully and though she had a game knee, she didn't limp all that much. Her greyish hair was tied in a neat bun and she wore no makeup on her wrinkled but delicate face. Laugh lines had carved small channels down her cheeks and when she laughed, which was quite often, tears would roll down them in small rivulets. She wasn't fat but you could call her dumpy—in a matronly way. Her grey plaid skirt fell gently down to her knees and a pink cardigan covered her silk blouse which was buttoned at the neck. She was quite prim and could seem forbidding and hard to those who didn't know her.

The picture postcards had been kept neatly tied by a blue ribbon in a chest of drawers. Miss Lewis opened the ribbon and showed the cards to Kamlesh. They were of scenes from various parts of Paris and its landmarks. The pictures of pavement artists, girls selling flowers, and couples sitting on the banks of the Seine watching a barge float by, brought back memories of happier times to Kamlesh. Tears welled in her eyes but she kept her composure and Miss Lewis pretended she hadn't noticed.

Instead she reached for a brown bag and took out some sweets. 'Here, have one of these. It's from stickjaw country,' Miss Lewis said.

It was an old ploy and nearly all the girls who had gone to meet Miss Lewis had at some time or the other got a stickjaw, hard toffee made by Kwality's in Doon. Once you had it in your mouth, you had a tough time talking because the caramel would bind your teeth together. It was Miss Lewis's way of keeping you quiet for a while. It always worked.

Kamlesh sucked on it and remembered flavours from days gone by. She remembered all the good times she and the girls had while growing up. The records they were allowed to listen to in Miss Lewis's little cottage and the way she had taught them to waltz and foxtrot. 'It will come in handy girls one day ... and one, two, three ...' she intoned to the sound of the *Blue Danube* or the more rapid beat of Dorsey's band.

'And how is your pretty sister, Pappi?' Miss Lewis asked.

'Not good at all. Not good. You wouldn't recognise her if you saw her now,' Kamlesh replied.

'But why? What happened to her? Has she got the flu?' Miss Lewis said with concern in her voice.

But that was just a show. Miss Lewis had known for a very long time about Pappi's affair with Kukku. She had a chain of dedicated informers—or gossipmongers, if you will—who allowed her to keep a fingertip) on the pulse of the town. There was very little that happened in Mansuri that didn't find its way to Miss Lewis, especially if it involved any of her past students. And this, when she rarely stirred out of the convent. But she didn't want to hurt Kamlesh's sensibilities.

'Well it's a long story but I will make it short. Pappi says she is in love with our cousin Kukku. Do you remember him? You do? She wants to marry him. Papaji has had offers from other people and has suggested she take one of those. But she is adamant. For the last three months she has locked herself in her room. She doesn't go for walks nor does she talk to anyone, including me. We don't know what to do,' Kamlesh said.

Miss Lewis hadn't said a word all the time Kamlesh went on about her family's problems. Kamlesh had also talked about how her future as a designer was now jeopardised as she had left her studies midway to be home to give support to her mother and father. What she didn't confide to Miss Lewis was her affair with Jean Paul, a Frenchman.

The reason for that was quite simple. There was no future in it. There was no way her parents would give their assent to the union. At the best, she could live with him while she was in Paris. But there was no way she could marry him and still be a part of her small family. The very thought of telling them the truth frightened her. There was every chance her father would have a stroke and her mother something similar. That was something she wouldn't dream of doing to her parents.

'I know something about matters of the heart,' Miss Lewis said instinctively, in her soft voice. 'It is best to let things go. By this I mean Pappi should go ahead with her plans, for better or worse. By denying her this small and, I must say, transitory pleasure, you will make a ghost of her. I wonder if your parents will even understand romantic love. I know they are conservative and traditionalists.'

Kamlesh nodded because there was nothing she could say to Miss Lewis. It was pointless telling her that her parents were intransigent to the extent that they would rather see Pappi dead than married to Kukku. As a matter of fact, she knew that if she broke the news about her love life with a foreigner and non-Sikh, it would be enough to drive them to suicide.

Miss Lewis continued in her soft voice, 'You see, Kamlesh dear, we all have a quota of happiness ordained to us by God. Some of us use it up early, some of us in the middle years and very few in our dotage. I should know.'

Miss Lewis knew it very well. She had been sixteen when she fell in love with a dashing sergeant in the army. Her father, an engine driver with the Peninsular Railway, lived in Kharagpur's railway colony. The soldier, Rodney Gardner, came to visit his uncle there on his annual leave. The two were cousins, and getting the family to agree to a wedding was out of the question. The next best thing was to elope—which they did. They landed up in Agra where they were married by a sympathetic priest. Soon, Rodney had to leave to join his regiment which was being shipped overseas to take part in the fighting in Mesopotamia. Miss Lewis, then known as Roselyn Gardner, was pregnant when Rodney set sail from Bombay.

Rodney left some money with Roselyn and promised to send her more every month. It was a promise he couldn't keep because death silenced him forever. Roselyn, now a war widow and prominently pregnant, wrote to the regiment, explaining her predicament. The colonel of the regiment was unable to help as the marriage hadn't received official sanction, and Rodney's family pension was sent to his mother. With no way to earn any money, and carrying a child, Roselyn returned home where her understanding father forgave her for running away and welcomed her back. But her mother was unforgiving. She told Roselyn she could stay there as long as she was pregnant but once she had had her 'bastard', she was to leave.

And that was that. So much for Christian charity and compassion. The child was handed over to an orphanage and Roselyn, now Miss Roselyn Lewis, fetched up in the convent in Mansuri where she began work as a matron. She endeared herself to the nuns with her capacity to work hard, and over time, finished the studies required to be a full-fledged teacher. Her happiness lay in the future of her students and from that source she got her supply of unlimited joy.

Over the years she had become a legend and attained an almost iconic status. She had quite forgotten the short-lived marriage and the baby that she had given birth to. But when she thought about it, which was rarely, she wondered about her child. Then, a sad look would mask her face and she would shrug her shoulders and get on with her life. She never left the convent to go home to Kharagpur and as far as her parents were concerned, she was dead. In the early days she did get an occasional postcard from her father but she never replied. She had buried the ghosts of her youth.

'But Miss Lewis, Pappi can't go ahead. Unless my parents agree, Kukku's won't. My father wants her to marry a man in a better position. Not another shopkeeper. That's the way these days. He would like her to marry a professional and not a businessman,' Kamlesh said.

'That is something that we would all like. But I think that we don't always get what we want. It's like the government. People get the government they deserve. Parents get the children they deserve. And children get the parents they deserve. I know,' Miss Lewis said, and Kamlesh sensed the sadness deep in her heart.

They talked about this and that, drank cups of tea and when the school bell rang for supper Miss Lewis said she had to go up to the dining room to see that the children ate their food properly. Kamlesh said she had to get back home, and the two parted with a warm embrace. Walking home, Kamlesh realised that nothing had been resolved. And with that knowledge rankling her, she walked into Cliff Hall.

❦

SIX

Kukku had come back to Mansuri after his winter sojourn in Bombay. He had gone to Cliff Hall from where he was turned away at the door and told to never come back. It was Kamlesh who had to do that bit of dirty work and a mystified Kukku told his parents about the strange behaviour. From being a very welcome visitor he was now an outsider. His parents, who had been keeping up with the gossip, knew all about Pappi's retreat and depression. When you have servants in the house nothing ever remains a secret for long. They told Kukku about the ban on Pappi from stepping out of the house and how she had locked herself in her room and was not seeing anyone. Kukku was a sensitive sort and took all this to heart.

In a fit of desperation he barged into Cliff Hall at a time when Papaji had gone to the shop and Kamlesh was doing some errands in town. There was only Mummyji, who was Kukku's aunt, in the house. Brushing her aside he knocked on the door to Pappi's room.

'It's me, Kukku,' he said.

There was no response from inside. Kukku knocked again and pleaded with Pappi to open the door.

After a while he heard someone moving around. Then the bolt was drawn and the door opened. When he saw Pappi he felt weak at the knees and had to lean against the door to hold himself up. He thought he was looking at a ghost. Pappi appeared to be floating in space. Her pale, almost white, skin was drawn taut across her face, dark shadows had formed under her eyes and it appeared that if a strong gust of wind came along she would be blown off like a dry leaf. She looked at Kukku, her big eyes almost grotesque in her hollowed face. They held no expression and the luminosity that marked them in days gone by had disappeared. Her hair had been reduced to a crop and had not been washed or combed for days. It formed an untidy mop on top of her head.

Kukku, unable to bear the sight, turned away and ran out blindly from Cliff Hall. Mummyji collapsed in a chair. Just then, Kamlesh walked in. She gently guided Pappi back to her bed and closed the door.

Then she turned on her mother and said with bitterness in her voice, 'Are you satisfied?'

Papaji was summoned from the shop and after a brief conference it was decided to send the sisters to the house of a relative in Nainital. This quaint little town is set high in the hills around a lake formed in an extinct volcano. In spring and summer it is quite enjoyable for healthy and normal people. But Pappi wasn't at all well. She had to be carried in a 'dandy' every morning for an outing around the lake. Bundled in thick blankets, her pale face just visible, she was carried by two men in the hammock-like contraption while Kamlesh followed on foot.

The fresh air from the lake and the deodar-scented breeze from the dense forest around the lake began to work their wonders. Pappi regained her appetite and began to eat regular meals. She was able to totter around the house and after some time managed to walk by herself to the lawn to bask in the brilliant sun. The combination of sunshine and fresh air, regular meals and loving and tender care by Kamlesh saw Pappi's ravaged body come to life. Broken hearts sometimes mend as fast as they break.

Two months later, Kamlesh was able to report to her parents that Pappi was quite normal and ready to come home. But the parents had different ideas on the subject. They asked her to take Pappi to Simla, another hill station and the former summer capital of India. There Pappi joined a college for further studies and spent the next three years away from Mansuri except for brief visits during college vacations. Kukku, on the rebound, married a rich man's daughter and set up his business in Delhi.

Kamlesh saw it was pointless to go back to Paris. She heard from Jean Paul but she didn't reply to his letters, and after a time, they stopped coming. Kamlesh was now involved in her father's work which she expanded to do business with shops in the plains. From all appearances, she appeared quite content, but there was an air about her of abstraction, of being too involved in her work, and she had neither the time nor the inclination to socialise. She had no friends to speak of and, unlike most other women, didn't spend her time in idle gossip. Her father and mother suggested marriage a couple of times but she refused pointblank and the subject was never brought up again.

Kamlesh kept visiting Miss Lewis from time to time to tell her how Pappi was doing. In a sense,

Miss Lewis was her only true friend in whom she could confide. Like most lonely and reserved people, Kamlesh ploughed a lonely furrow on the social landscape of Mansuri. She grew her flowers, like most people do when they have gardens, but with little love or enthusiasm. She drifted into more esoteric interests in which she communicated only with what she liked to believe was God. It is a difficult terrain and many who have tried to navigate it have fallen by the wayside. It is the fortunate few who find the ideal balance—and Kamlesh wasn't yet one of them. But she strived nevertheless.

⸻ ◦/◦/◦ ⸻

SEVEN

One day a man claiming to be 'Bhagwan' came to Mansuri and set himself up in a neat little cottage. In the style of godmen everywhere, he had a large entourage of followers. His real name, before he donned the mantle of godship, was Sudip Biswas. He was born near Hooghly, an industrial town on the opposite bank of the river Hooghly. Opposite from Calcutta, that is. Sudip Biswas grew up like any other boy. Played football, chased the girls around Puja time and in general was as normal as could be. He failed his high school examination, for which he was roundly thrashed by his schoolteacher father—again, quite normal, because boys expected to get thrashed when they failed the all-important board examination. The result of the beating was that he ran away from home and found himself on the first night at the gates of the R.K. Mission in nearby Belur.

The Rama Krishna Mission was founded by Rama Krishna, another man who left home to discover the truth. In his search for truth he travelled all over northern India. He met various people, saw many things and—as travellers are wont to—broadened his intellectual horizons. He then preached for many years and built up a massive following of educated and rich people. They in turn spread his message far and wide and the R.K. Mission was established, running schools and hospitals, among other things.

That night, as Sudip Biswas huddled outside the gate of the massive mansion that housed the mission, he was approached by another youth. They sat together for a while. In the beginning there was nothing much to say. They looked at each other and grunted in acknowledgment of each other's presence. It was getting on to night and a stiff breeze from the Hooghly blew their way and they shivered in the unexpected cold. They dozed off and on and, around midnight, were suddenly wide awake when they were joined by another man.

This man was middle-aged and dressed in nothing but his underwear. He had risen from the banks of the river like an apparition and, silhouetted against the night fog, frightened the two young men. For a long time he stood motionless in front of them. Then his knees seemed to buckle under him and he collapsed. He lay in front of them, motionless.

The only sound around them was the lapping of the small waves of the ebbing tide against the bank. Occasionally, they heard the hooting of a river tug and the phut-phut of its engine as it made it way upstream towards the cantonment of Barrackpore. The night passed uneasily for the two of them. They didn't want to know if the man lying in front of them was dead or alive. Petrified with fear they sat on their haunches, their bodies shivering from the cold of the night. Just as the false dawn broke and the first of the early morning bathers streamed past them, the gates of the mission were thrown open.

The man who opened the gate looked at the two obviously destitute boys and then at the semi-naked form of the man lying in front of them. He came and touched the man with the toe of his foot. There was no movement. He then knelt down and felt his pulse.

'This man is alive,' he observed. 'You two help me lift him up and carry him inside.'

They lifted the man and, carrying him, followed the man inside the mission. He led them to a room on the ground floor and asked them to lay the man down on a bench. In the light of an electric bulb he examined the man dispassionately. Then he went away and returned with another man. The second man had a stethoscope around his neck and he used it to check the man's heartbeat.

After probing around he said, 'Nothing to worry about. He'll come around. By the way, where did he come from?'

Sudip, now in the middle of two obviously alive and reasonable men, was the first to open his mouth. 'He came out of the river, sirs,' he muttered.

'And where did you two come from?' the man who looked like a doctor asked.

The boys said nothing. They sat on their haunches, eyes downcast.

The two men then left them and after a while they saw the man from the river open his eyes. He blinked at the naked light bulb and then looked around. He tried to speak but no sound came from his throat and he lay there flat on his back, his paunch heaving with the effort of breathing. He tried to get up but couldn't. Like a big, beached Ganga river dolphin, the man breathed in deep grunts, and the two boys thought he was about to give up the ghost.

The man lay on the bench, his eyes wide open, staring at the roof. His breathing was slowly coming back to normal and as the morning light seeped into the room the boys saw a big bruise on the man's chest. Clotted blood had formed on his nose. The man who had brought them inside came back with a kettle of tea and three kullars. He poured tea into the small mud cups and passed them around. Except to the man with the bruise on his chest.

The doctor came back and examined the man some more. After a while he told the other man, 'Looks like another attempted suicide. See these bruises and the dried-up blood. Looks like he jumped off the Vivekananda Bridge and survived. No broken bones, as far as I can make out. Let's get him to the x-ray room.'

The boys carried the man to the x-ray room. He was laid out on a table and the doctor fiddled with some knobs overhead, lowered the camera and took a few x-rays. After a while he examined the plates, grunted to himself and told the other man, 'Remarkable. Not one broken bone. The man should have been dead. No one survives a fall from the bridge. Unless he is an expert swimmer.'

'God's will,' the other man said, and accompanied the doctor out. The two boys, now alone with the patient, looked at each other.

'What should we do?' asked Sudip.

His companion of the night, who seemed to know the routine inside the mission, said, 'Come with me. They serve breakfast to beggars in the kitchen.'

A line of bedraggled people had begun to form at the kitchen by the time the boys reached there. They joined it and as it moved briskly along, they found themselves finally at its head. They were served luchis and dal. Sudip remembered the semi-casualty in the x-ray room and asked the serving man for another helping for a friend. The man shooed him off—with an expletive to help him on his way.

Sudip and the other boy, whose name was Shankar—they had exchanged names while waiting for their turn in the food line—went back to the x-ray room. The man was lying where they had left him. Sudip offered his plantain leaf to the man and signalled him to help himself to some food. The man continued to stare at the ceiling. Shankar gingerly inserted a piece of luchi between his lips. It was like putting food into a dead man's mouth. The man neither chewed nor swallowed it. The piece of luchi just stayed there.

The boys retreated to a corner and ate their meal without a sound. After finishing their food they took the empty (emptied) plantain leaves and deposited them in a garbage container outside. They looked around the well-laid out grounds of the mission and admired the flowers. The sun had come out in all its fury and though it was still early morning the boys felt its heat.

'Time to move on,' Shankar said.

'Where?' Sudip asked.

'Oh, I don't know. I am just a wanderer. I think I'll go along the river to whereever it begins,' Shankar said.

The two boys went to say goodbye to the man from the river. He didn't respond and so the boys just left him as he was, and moved away and out of the mission gates. No one stopped them and they made it to the main road. Once out of the mission they looked back and were startled to see the semi-naked man following them. He still had the piece of luchi in his mouth and was shakily making his way towards them. He tripped once but managed to hold himself upright, and came and stood before them.

'Go back, man. You'll be well looked after at the mission,' Shankar told him.

The man stayed where he was. The boys noticed for the first time how incongruously obese he was. In the light of day Shankar appeared to be a well-built young man, with long hair and a wisp of a beard. He was wearing a lungi and a vest and was barefoot. On his right shoulder hung a cloth bag which contained a gaamcha, a kind of multi-purpose piece of cloth which served as a turban or could be used to towel up after a bath. There was a thick book that he kept covered in another piece of cloth. And that was all. Compared to what Sudip had it was quite a lot. Sudip just had a shirt and the trousers he was wearing when he left home and a pair of rubber shoes. He also had secreted away in a 'chor' pocket two hundred rupees in ten-rupee notes.

The boys looked at the fat man and wondered what to do with him. When they walked, he walked with them. If they stopped, he too stopped. It was like they had picked up a stray dog or a shadow that insisted on following them wherever they went. By noon the trio had reached a small village on the highway. They saw a teashop in a shanty and Shankar walked upto it.

There were some people sitting on benches waiting for a bus. He began to beg from them. It was all a matter of style, he explained later to Sudip. He would simply go and stand in front of a person and put out a hand, palm upwards. His eyes would be fixed on the man's and he wouldn't say a word. Either the man would look away or pretend to do something or he would reach in his pocket and drop some change in his outstretched palm.

By the time the bus came and the people boarded it, Shankar had collected a total of eight annas. That was what an unskilled labourer earned in a day. He bought a loaf of bread and a cube of butter and gave half of each to Sudip.

'Eat,' he ordered.

As an afterthought he offered some to the fat man. No response. The luchi was still there, neatly tucked away in one corner like a paan. Shankar shrugged and ate the bread and butter. Then he went to the hand pump next to the shop and drank his fill of water. They had been sitting in the shade of a sprawling banyan and without much fuss Shankar stretched out and went to sleep. Sudip followed his example and curled up next to him. The fat man sat on his haunches and just stared into the emptiness.

EIGHT

The trio progressed up the Gangetic plain. Most days they slept out in the open under a tree. Sometimes they strayed into old ruins. At times they sheltered from the monsoon that was following them in structures built along the river's cremation ghaats. There they watched the mortal remains of strangers being reduced to ashes that were then flung into the river. They weren't the only people on the road. Mendicants of all types trudged alongside. So did street performers, magicians and travelling salesmen.

When they came in sight of bigger towns they found their way to the nearest dharamshala where they were allowed to curl up in a corner. In the first few days Shankar had been doing the begging and getting the food. Sudip picked up his style and in no time lost his hesitancy to beg. The fat man had by now become a thin man. Sudip had bought him a lungi and a vest, which he accepted changing into, but they had not been able to get a word out of him. He sometimes ate the food proffered by the boys. Mostly, he ate nothing.

The boys had wondered about the man's past. Sudip had told Shankar all about himself and Shankar, who had had a more colourful past, talked freely about it. He had been abandoned by his parents as a little boy. They had left him in their little hut while they went scrounging for food during a famine that followed widespread flooding of the countryside. In turn, he too became a scrounger and found his way to the big city of Calcutta where he lived on the streets along with other boys his age. He learnt the art of being a pickpocket from a man called Ustaad. But the man kept all his earnings and only gave him enough to buy some food. One day, he broke free and ran away. He joined another gang in another part of the city and over the years he too became an ustaad and operated his own gang. One day the law caught up with him and he was sent to the Alipore Jail for six months. When he met Shankar he had just come out of jail.

The older man was an enigma. The boys tried to figure out something about him, his background and why he was following them. When they had first seen him he looked like a man who had done no manual work in his life. His feet were as soft as a baby's and he obviously wore shoes before he jumped or was thrown into the river. His fingernails had been cut short, he had a proper haircut and was clean-shaven. His body bore no scars except for the big bruise which he presumably got when he made contact with the water. And the only piece of garment on his body, a pair of boxer shorts, was made of fine cotton. They had dressed him up in a lungi and a vest and bought a pair of rubber chappals because of the blisters on his feet. Now, after a couple of months on the road, he was no longer recognisable as the man who came out of the river. He had a longish salt-and-pepper beard, his long hair was tied in a knot, and his paunch had gone. Since he didn't speak they began to call him 'Moni Baba', the sadhu who has sworn to be silent.

They had an enjoyable break at a place called Allahabad where the Magh Mela was on in full swing and millions of devotees had collected at the Sangam—the point on the Gangetic plain where the Ganga, the Jamuna and the mythical Saraswati meet at the place called Triveni. There these pilgrims wash away their accumulated sins in one big go—or so they believe.

The three lingered there, along with thousands of sadhus, perhaps the biggest gathering of unemployed, unemployable and unwilling-to-work men in one place.

By the end of winter and just when spring was making its first footmarks in the plains, they reached the foothills at a place called Rishikesh. This was the gateway to the Himalayas. Here, thousands of devotees began their long march to the shrines of Kedarnath and Badrinath. En route there were a number of other spots considered to be holy.

It was at one of these spots that the three of them met the guru who was to change the course of their lives.

Under his stern instructions, several years of penance and long periods of meditation followed, which taught them that 'moksha' was freedom from births and deaths. The guru told them that this was the way to attain eternal bliss that is measured in neither space nor time. They were convinced that they were destined to attain moksha and final freedom.

With time they learnt to kill their ego after trying to answer the question: Who am I? That was the net result of a school of meditation called Koham Dhyana. Who am I?

They began to dress in the saffron robes of sadhus and carried wooden begging bowls. Matted hair and long beards completed their personae as holy men and their guru then unleashed them on an unsuspecting world.

By now they had completely shed their previous identities. The middle-aged man, after all those years of meditation and yoga, looked like a youth, but he still didn't speak a word. He was introduced as the Moni Baba and his spokesman was Sudip, who gave his name as Swami Vishwanandaji.

As for Shankar, he left them for another guru who was a repository of many secrets of tantra and its various rituals. Shankar disappeared with him somewhere in the high altitude valleys of the Garhwal Himalayas only to re-appear towards the end of this story.

After attaining the level of 'diksha'—being initiated into the guru's confidence by letting him whisper the magical mantra in their ears—the remaining two went out in the world to spread the message of moksha. They travelled all over the north of the country and finally returned to big and ramshackle Allahabad, where they rented a small building in the congested Alopi Bagh area to house their ashram. Allahabad was a natural choice. Because of its holy location in the heartland of the Gangetic plain, it made sound business sense to set up an ashram for all those lost and confused souls who chose to drop anchor there.

In the beginning, they had few devotees. Vishwanandaji's evening sermons lacked the fire to ignite his followers' imaginations. Moni Baba sat alongside him and never said a word although he conducted all the rituals to perfection.

One day, a young woman devotee, a widow who had been turned out of her husband's house after the young man died in an accident, reached the ashram and set up her bedroll at Swamiji's feet. She was a slim and soft-faced woman who took on the ashram's running chores without being asked. She cooked and cleaned and in turn got two meals a day and a roof to sleep under. Swamiji also provided her with two cotton saris and matching blouses every year, and the arrangement continued for some years.

She was given the name of Saraswati, the goddess

of learning, and all who came to the ashram called her Behenji. With her coming the ashram's popularity spread wider and the number of devotees increased exponentially. This, coupled with a reputation Moni Baba had somehow acquired as a man who could help childless couples to conceive, helped, and in time he became the main attraction at the ashram.

Another man joined the ashram and soon became an indispensable asset. He managed the financial and other administrative affairs. Everybody called him called Babuji.

⸺◦◦◦⸺

NINE

This story could not be told without taking extracts from Babuji's diary which was written in Hindi and sometimes English—and later recovered by the police in raids on the ashram to collect evidence against Babuji. The writer has taken liberties with the translation and grammar to make the account readable. It is nevertheless as close to the truth as is possible.

Babuji's diary:

I was among some others attracted to Swamiji. Forced to resign after a few years of service as a bureaucrat because I had been caught with my hand in the till, I was at a loose end until I drifted into Allahabad, a place known for the unscrupulous, the thugs and all those looking to disappear without a trace in the humbug called religion and spirituality. I chanced to read about Bhagwan—as he had begun to be called—in a local paper and it was then that I decided to leave my nagging and ugly wife and wastrel son to don the saffron robes of a mendicant.

I found in Swamiji a guru worth emulating and soon became a member of his inner circle by donating a part of my ill-gotten gains to Swamiji's coffers. My name used to be P.P. Sharma—though no one calls me that anymore. I am now simply Babuji. And I have disappeared from my earlier life. It was, in a sense, the perfect camouflage, the kind a tiger looks for in a dense jungle.

Over the years I had amassed a major fortune from 'nazranas' for favours done to various people, and a large part of it I put at Swamiji's disposal. This was the safest way to get the money back into circulation and out of the grubby paws of my wife and others interested in doing me in for corruption. The finances of the ashram were, generally speaking, a mess, and I began to build up a treasure trove.

It was at my urging that Swamiji began to dress in fine silks, wear flashing diamond rings and a heavy gold necklace, and Moni Baba shed his commonplace cotton orange shift for rather attractive ankle-length silk gowns and a solid gold Rolex. This business of ashrams is like theatre. You have to catch the attention of the unwary suckers that throng places like these looking for something, anything. In their ignorance they fall for the glitter and razzmatazz— as the Americans describe show business—as the real thing. And then they are trapped. This is my view, and cynical as it is, it is nevertheless true. As true as most things in this world of 'maya'—illusion.

I changed a lot of things at the ashram. The austere lifestyle gave way to sumptuous feasts. A larger place was acquired to house the increasing number of devotees. Behenji moved into the large silver-plated four-poster bed of Swamiji and, as it happens when people share the same bed, she became pregnant and gave birth to a healthy son.

Swamiji began to travel to various cities where his appearance was preceded by the pomp and show associated with a circus coming to town. Days before his arrival at each of these places, I would land up and check into the best hotel in town and orchestrate a parade through the town with elephants, horses and camels all richly caparisoned, accompanied by marching brass bands. Posters would be pasted all over the town accompanied by advertisements in local newspapers extolling people to come and listen to Swamiji. Suitable grounds would be booked— generally the parade ground which exists in nearly every small town in India—which I, with my influence, and the usual bribe, was able to secure free from the administration.

At that time it was my understanding, unspoken of course, that I was the fundraiser and collector for the ashram. That was quite easily done. I knew an endless number of colleagues who had amassed fortunes from one scam or the other, many politicians who had done the same and all of them wanted to see their money giving them a return which would not attract too much attention. A secret donation to the ashram entitled them to a return on their investment which otherwise would have been frozen capital. And there was nobody to ask uncomfortable questions.

We bought a linotype press, hired compositors and began publishing the speeches of Swamiji. Besides increasing the number of devotees, we found a legitimate way to recycle the sleaze money given to us as donations—and I was able to organise affairs in such a way that no one would raise an eyebrow. In the first ten years we had enough money to open three schools, a rural hospital equipped with the best equipment and manned by doctors, some of them with shady backgrounds, who needed to be sheltered by us, and the usual complement of nurses and other support staff. I also arranged for the necessary publicity for such 'good works'.

Of course, Swamiji was kept in the loop but in rather vague terms. Firstly he didn't want to know the details. They were too taxing and he would say, with a tired look on his face, 'Babuji, this is your department. You run it.' But Moni Baba seemed to be quite familiar with the accounting process and demanded to see the books. Initially, I thought the man couldn't know much. I had no idea of his background, or the circumstances under which he had joined up with Swamiji, and was therefore quite taken aback when he saw through my various machinations and manipulations. I knew I had to watch out for him.

The other task I was asked to handle was the education of Swamiji's illegitimate son by Behenji. The young boy showed some intellectual promise and I advised Swamiji that the best course of action was to send him abroad to one of the English public schools. Swamiji agreed. He was too engrossed in his prayers and sermons to pay too much attention to his son's future. Since I had a free hand in the matter I arranged for the boy to be admitted to Eton in England, and off he went, to return only five years later a much more sophisticated man ready to take on the world.

He was called Sanjay Dutt. I had, as a precautionary measure, sodomised the young boy to cow his spirit, and to ensure his slavelike devotion to me, made sure he only got his allowances after he did what I bade him to.

Except for the inner circle no one knew the truth

about Swamiji's son. The word was that he was a nephew who Swamiji had adopted and that he would be the eventual heir.

Nobody questioned Sanjay's thorough English education and lifestyle. When he came back from England he had developed a taste for the good life. He smoked imported cigarettes and liked his glass of whisky.

Since he didn't want to live in the ashram, I checked him into the best hotel in town called Barnett's, which was in the Civil Lines area and quite separated from the dirty, claustrophobic and congested area of Alopi Bagh. Here he could spend his time in air-conditioned comfort. He had also become a raging homosexual and would often bring his English lovers to India. I was the beneficiary of all this in that I too participated in the orgies we had far away from the ashram in the cool luxury of a hotel room.

It was then that I hit upon the idea that we should spend the hot summer months at a hill station. I made inquiries and decided Mansuri would suit us fine. It was the place where India's maharajahs and business tycoons liked to spend the summer. We rented a big bungalow that would amply accommodate the usual coterie of followers, servants, cooks and so on. Swamiji had no objections and said it was a good idea as he would be close to the Himalayas again. Moni Baba nodded his agreement.

We booked a special train to take us to the valley

town from where Mansuri was an hour's drive away. An advance party had reached there and the usual reception was organised. Curious people asked who the dignitary was and they were told he was Bhagwanji, the God who walked the earth. They were invited to listen to his 'parvachans'—pure thoughts. Within a day of our settling down in Mansuri the bungalow was besieged by hundreds of curious onlookers. Maharanis and rich women were the first to make a beeline to our bungalow.

Here I must mention that the Swamiji was a handsome man, with a striking voice and piercing looks. Women found themselves attracted to him and his reputation had already spread to Mansuri by the time we reached there. Understandably, there were long lines of such women waiting to touch his feet and get his blessings. I decided that we should celebrate Swamiji's birthday in right royal style. No one knew his real date of birth so I cooked up an imaginary one and all the faithful were told to assemble on a particular day to take part in a birthday procession.

The procession meandered its way through the hill town accompanied by the usual complement of a marching band and women throwing flower petals in the path of Bhagwanji's rickshaw that was pulled by five men in fine livery. The man himself sat dressed in his best finery and jewels. I had designed a turban studded with an appropriate number of gems and his feet were shod in slippers embroidered with gold thread. In his left hand he held a golden mace. His women disciples walked along, whisking away flies. Two attendants sprinkled rose water all round to kill the stench of horse manure. Men armed with spears and shotguns and dressed in medieval uniforms rode local ponies with the air of an armed escort.

We made a great impression on the tourists in Mansuri and the local population. Our bills with the local suppliers were enough to keep the greedy shopkeepers in profit for the rest of the year. At least a hundred people ate in the temporary ashram every day and 'prasad' was made for hundreds more who came to listen to 'Bhagwan' in the evenings. Our booklets on Bhagwan's teachings were outrageously priced but even then they sold like hot cakes. The small stock that I brought with me finished in the first week. I promptly ordered another lot from our headquarters in Allahabad.

Initially, our booklets were in Hindi but soon I realised that printing them in English would bring better dividends. In the English edition I did a bit of innovation. I thought I was a rather good poet and since I had never been published (the few publishers I showed my poems rejected them out of hand) I would from time to time slip in my own poems and pass them off as the work of Bhagwan. I couldn't resist the overriding desire to see my work in print even though I knew I was cheating.

Cheating had been a way of life with me for nearly the ten-odd years that I worked for the government. It is difficult to shed a regular habit, bad though it may be. Ask any smoker or alcoholic. I had lost all scruples and as the manager of all the funds at the ashram, I had quite a lot of money at my command and no need to account for it. I started salting away small amounts for the inevitable rainy day. I knew that, one day, Swamiji's bastard would come of age and take over control. Then there was Moni Baba who, without saying a word, would give me looks that branded me a thief and a swindler. This Moni Baba intrigued me and I set about finding out something of his past.

The first season in Mansuri proved quite profitable and after the rains we decided to move back to the plains where life had become much more livable. Winter there is the season when people seem to have all the time for following spiritual pursuits. I made detailed travel plans and booked a special train to take us around the country. The train took us everywhere and as our fame spread people flocked to our prayer meetings in droves. Soon we were only visiting the big cities and people were forced to visit our camps from the neighbouring towns and countryside.

Around this time I introduced another innovation to collect more funds. We would set up a mela, or fair, wherever we went. Shops would be rented out to those who wanted to sell their wares. Needless to say, there was a mad rush to book these stalls. There were all kinds of entertainers and tradesmen—magicians, men selling homemade cures to all kinds of ailments, small-time film exhibitors who showed the latest hits from Bombay in their tents and, on the quiet, a brothel or two under my direct supervision. Ostensibly, these brothels were where dancing girls performed to entertain the crowds but after nightfall they became quiet places for releasing the libido. And there was also the money to be made from the sale of cheap liquor. Again, directly under my control.

There was no way that news of any of my side operations would ever reach the ears of Swamiji or Moni Baba. Nobody had access to them without my permission and this meant that nobody could talk to them unless I was present.

Some people who were big donors were allowed to have brief chats with Swamiji or what we used to call private 'darshans'. I was assisted in my endeavours by one of my old personal assistants who had known me virtually for my entire period of service in the government and was well acquainted with my devious ways. I could trust him implicitly. He too had left his wife and family and joined the caravan, so to speak.

—◦◦◦—

TEN

Among the thousands who visited Bhagwan's Mansuri ashram were Kamlesh and Pappi, and their father accompanied them like a faithful shadow. In actual fact he wanted to keep an eye on them because he had very little faith and trust in self-proclaimed holy men.

Initially, they were simply part of the crowd. One day, Babuji spotted the sisters and their father and invited them to sit up close to Bhagwan. Soon, they had a regular place at the feet of the Swami. Babuji had noticed Pappi's beauty and was convinced that there was something to be made of it. One day he invited the two sisters to Bhagwan's bedroom, a very rare privilege. There they were made to sit at his feet and had the privilege of a private conversation. One assumes they posed the various questions that bothered their mortal beings and Swamiji gave them the right kind of answers.

Swamiji's son Sanjay Dutt would often drop in to visit his mother and father. He too noticed Pappi and soon a conversation was struck up. Pappi was very impressed by Sanjay's English, his style of dressing (he always wore three-piece suits with button-down collars and double cuffs) and his intellectual reach (he read *The Economist*, et al). They soon found they had some common interests and Sanjay asked Pappi to join him for coffee in a local restaurant where an espresso machine had just been installed. The machine was the first of its kind in the small hill town and it was quite the done thing to be seen having espresso there.

Pappi's father did not like this one bit. He was dead set against the whole idea. But he was helpless because he could not exercise his will anymore. His feeble efforts to control his daughters were met with obdurate references to his old-fogeyness, and the counter-advice that he should stick to his prayers and that kind of stuff. The mother had, a long time ago, stopped having a say in the affairs of the sisters.

Pappi had recovered from her heartbreak. She was living quite a normal life. She too had joined her sister in the family business and was a great help in selecting designs, yarn and colours. They had extended their line of work and were designing woollen garments for women and children. In addition they had an understanding with Oxfam, which was buying the garments made by their team of women workers, for eventual export to its headquarters in London.

On the family front, the mother and father of Kamlesh and Pappi had more or less left the running of the business to the sisters. Papaji had become more and more engrossed in spiritual matters.

Mummyji was bedridden after a stroke and was more or less a vegetable who had to be washed and fed by one or other of the sisters.

There was no longer talk of marriage and romance, and passion seemed to have disappeared from the lives of the sisters. From all appearances it was as if these two rather exquisite women were doomed to lead the lives of spinsters and would never bear children or do any of the things people do when they marry. They had turned to religion for whatever spiritual solace it afforded them. Swamiji's appearance as Bhagwan in Mansuri had given them the opportunity to immerse themselves in godmanspeak. Their daily lives were centred around the activities at the ashram and soon people noticed that the two of them enjoyed the complete confidence of Babuji.

Some people also noticed Pappi and Sanjay together on their long walks which were more or less becoming a regular feature. Initially, Pappi was accompanied by Kamlesh but by the end of that season Kamlesh had dropped off and the two of them were alone in their meanderings around the hill station.

But, like in all small towns, there was the town gossip. He was a eunuch and midwife. Nothing worth knowing escaped him and he would regale local people with all kinds of delicious tidbits of information, particularly the much appreciated sexual practices of the town's denizens. He had nicknames for the more important people—such as the mayor, his mistress, and the padres and nuns who ran most of the English-medium schools. Lower down the order were the peccadilloes of the town's prominent shopkeepers. Since Mansuri could not boast of a brothel, most people hired women from the bigger towns in the plains and kept them in rented bungalows for the summers. These kept women would often be passed off as distant cousins or in-laws and thus there was a certain amount of legitimacy to their presence. But Banoo, the eunuch, saw through these shams. And as it happened, the fast-developing 'affair' between Pappi and Sanjay didn't escape Banoo's notice either, and consequently, a greater part of the town got to know about it.

ELEVEN

One day, Bhagwan upped and left for the plains. His entourage followed and the house was shut down for the winter. That left Pappi and Kamlesh quite distraught. It also made them rework their daily schedule. Now that they didn't get to spend any time at the ashram they concentrated on their business.

Besides, Mummyji was taking up more of their time. She had become a total invalid and needed constant attention. Soon, winter was upon them and as the snow fell and a frozen silence descended on Cliff Hall, Mummyji went to sleep and never woke up.

Papaji, lost in his thoughts, didn't even know that his wife of sixty years had died. He watched the sisters organise the funeral from his rocking chair in the corner of the drawing room. As a disinterested spectator he didn't make any move to help—not that he could. Some neighbours and members of the Sikh community took the old lady to the cremation ghat and her ashes were then thrown in the Ganga.

Cliff Hall soon acquired the atmosphere of a mausoleum. The sisters began to avoid visitors to their home. The lone servant woman was packed off with a decent settlement and no outsider was allowed inside the house. In the beginning the phone rang at least once a day but now there was no one to call them as they never responded.

That winter was also the last for Papaji. There wasn't much to describe his life. It had been one of upheaval, lost hopes, hatred for most humans, and disappointments. Nobody could honestly say that he or she missed him in any way. He had never contributed to anyone's life. Even his own daughters joined the ranks of those who forgot all about him the moment his ashes were swept away in the Ganga.

~

Spring came, and the sisters began to take a fresh look around Cliff Hall. They decided to spruce it up and a contractor was called in to do the whitewash and minor repairs. Years of neglect had allowed cobwebs to form all over the house. The bathrooms needed refurbishment and the wooden frames of the windows a coat of fresh paint. Some panes had broken and were boarded up with cardboard. They too were replaced. Windows were left open during the day and the musty smell that was the hallmark of the house was driven away by the fresh breeze from the northwest.

A new entrant into the household was a stray who the sisters called Boy. He was loveable black mutt who was a cross between a sheepdog and a terrier. When he wanted, Boy could be an alert watchdog. But he chose to spend most of his time asleep in the corner that was once occupied by Papaji's rocking chair.

By the time the work on the house was completed Bhagwan and his entourage re-entered the town with the usual fanfare. Babuji sent a message to the sisters to come attend the regular evening sermons. It was just what they were waiting for. They were among the first people to arrive and were, as in the past, welcomed into Bhagwan's presence. Bhagwan told them about his travels during the winter. The sisters told him about the death of their parents. Bhagwan told them that death was only the freeing of man from his mortal coils and after that happened, the 'aatma' lived on and a human being gained moksha. The sisters couldn't have cared less for those words of wisdom.

They settled into the rhythm of the ashram. Pappi resumed her evening walks with Sanjay Dutt, Bhagwan's bastard son.

One day they went to see a film and that set the agenda for the coming days, a movie and a dance at the ballroom of the Savoy becoming part of their daily ritual. This growing relationship did not go unnoticed by Babuji. He was waiting and watching, hoping Sanjay would propose to her because he planned to gain substantially from their marriage, and he was going to aid and abet that plan to the best of his capabilities. After all, Sanjay did what he was told, or else . . .

The affair didn't escape the sharp eyes and ears of the town eunuch. But this time round he made the gossip spicier by adding all kinds of juice that had his listeners asking for more. Banoo would describe in lurid detail the shape and colour of Pappi's generous breasts and nipples as she, reportedly, offered them to Sanjay to be sucked and caressed. Banoo would enlarge on the theme till the younger of his male listeners would surreptitiously caress their erect penises.

—◦◦◦—

TWELVE

Notes from Babuji's diary:

I keenly followed the summer of happiness for Sanjay and Pappi. I knew that here was a chance of taking the greatest risk in my life. A union between the two would serve me in many ways. Mainly, because I thought Sanjay would lose interest in the day-to-day running of the ashram, busy as he would be as a married man. I could then continue with my system of management, and control every activity in the ashram. It was time for me to put my bureaucratic experience to full and rich use.

One of the first things you learn as a bureaucrat is to maintain the status quo. In the ashram's case the situation was quite simple and yet complicated. Simple, because I was the uncrowned king, the be-all and do-all. Complicated because there was a lot of money to control. The flow of money, though in my hands, was also monitored by the man known as Moni Baba. Since no one knew anything about him, and Bhagwan refused to talk about how he came to be associated with this mysterious and intriguing man, it was up to me to find out.

While I was working out my plans I proposed to Bhagwan that we should now buy or get the government to donate land to build an even bigger ashram befitting his status. As usual he agreed without a murmur. I immediately approached a former maharaja who was also a minister in the government and quite close to the Prime Minister. This man was a regular disciple and had often said that we should have a set-up in the capital so that more people could benefit from Bhagwan's teachings. I put the proposal to him and he moved the necessary papers. Lo and behold, we were granted for posterity about 100 acres of land right on the banks of the Jamuna in New Delhi. This was real wealth and I knew we had arrived. At least *I* was going to benefit from this move immensely.

I immediately had the land fenced off and employed architects to build me a temple that was a replica of what had once existed in Dwarka but was now buried under the sea off the coast of Gujarat. To do this we employed a French firm of divers to photograph the temple underwater from all angles and also to get us the required measurements. Someone suggested we get satellite pictures and we did that too. Soon our architects had enough material to begin designing the new structure.

In the meantime, landscapers came and laid out vast gardens, groves of ornamental and fruit-yielding trees and a large lake with fountains and ghats for people to bathe at. In one corner of the property we set up a large dairy farm so that the ashram would have its own supply of milk and milk products. Land had been earmarked to grow vegetables, cereals and other daily staples, and a small army of farmers worked the land as volunteers. As the work began on laying the foundations and building the main five-storeyed temple, I moved in so that I could supervise the work personally. A compact house had been built in keeping with the rest of the architecture for my personal use, and I had a private road leading to it which meant that I could come and go as I pleased without being seen by other people in the ashram. My house was shared by my trusted assistant and partner in crime, and I installed a new addition in the shape and form of a pretty sanyasin who also acted as a sort of public relations officer—but, in the main, looked after my sensual well-being.

There was no shortage of funds. The day I spread the word among the faithful and began passing around an artist's sketch of the projected temple, money for the ashram poured in in bagfuls. Some people donated gold, some jewellery and most cash. We were a rich organisation and I as usual kept a tithe of its funds for myself in my secret accounts.

The finished structure was shaped like a huge lotus, with 1,008 petals, and was made of pure white marble. The petals were symbolic of the many diversities in human consciousness.

Bhagwan and his consort were housed in a palatial house slightly away from the main temple. The house was surrounded by a high wall and had a large courtyard almost as big as a football field where devotees would assemble to hear the Bhagwan's sermons which he preached from an impressive throne set up in the balcony of his second-floor residence. Entry to the palace's inner quarters on the second floor could only be made by taking a lift. It was strictly regulated by me, and only a handful of people were allowed to come near Bhagwan. On the occasions Bhagwan had to leave the ashram to go somewhere, there was a helicopter standing by in a helipad built at the rear of the palace. But most of the time, it was I who used the helicopter.

I had been told by a foreign disciple that we should have closed-circuit television network. It would make it easier for devotees to get a good look at Bhagwan on big screens set up for the purpose. Since the technology wasn't available in India, I imported it. It was an instant hit and the number of visitors increased, coming not only to hear Bhagwan but also to see this miracle of technology.

Moni Baba had been following all this activity with keen interest and Bhagwan had made it clear to me that all accounts must be submitted to him every week. I did that dutifully, fully aware that there was no way Moni Baba would know the prices of cement, stones, marble and all the other building material. I was naturally scooping off the top. The contractors had to pay my commission in cash before they were commissioned. This money I transferred to a secret bank account in Switzerland through my usual channel.

⸺◦◦◦⸺

THIRTEEN

In Mansuri the sisters were sitting in what passed for their drawing room looking at pictures of the new ashram coming up on the banks of the Yamuna near New Delhi. The pictures had been sent by Sanjay, and the magnificence of the complex was brought out in vivid Kodakcolour.

'I think we should get these pictures framed and put up in our shop so that everyone can see them,' Kamlesh said.

Pappi thought it was a super idea and the sisters went down to the photographer's shop on the Mall and bought a dozen chrome-finished frames. Soon the pictures were on display, and visitors to the shop oohed and aahed at the opulence on display. Bhagwan's fame had spread far and wide, and it was known that the sisters' shop was the place in Mansuri to buy his tapes and publications. Right through the summer season dozens of people thronged the shop to buy copies of the Bhagwan's teachings which were still full of the rather insipid poetry of Babuji. But the devotees did not know that.

In between the sisters did brisk business as the devotees would invariably pick up a pullover or a cardigan or a baby suit or the specially designed scarves with Bhagwan's portrait embroidered on them.

The romance between Pappi and Sanjay progressed by leaps and bounds. Soon, a year had passed and Sanjay, at Babuji's goading and coaxing, thought it was time to pop the question. He came up to Mansuri in the autumn when the skies were blue and the grass couldn't have been greener. The sun shone benignly and the air was full of fragrance. It was the time of year for festivities and marriages and since nearly a year had passed after the death of their parents, the sisters were not averse to the idea of a wedding in the family. The two discussed Sanjay's proposal and thought he was the right sort for man for Pappi. He was well educated, had money and was passably good-looking. They didn't have to consult anyone else as there was no one they considered family, and the matter was quickly resolved.

Bhagwan married Sanjay and Pappi in a simple ceremony in Mansuri. The couple then set off for their honeymoon in Europe which took them to all the exotic destinations that Pappi had only dreamt about. Her postcards from Rome, Paris, London and Barcelona were, in those heady and early days, bubbly.

But Kamlesh soon began to detect that there was

something not right, as the postcards became more and more abrupt, and then, after a few weeks, stopped. Alarmed, Kamlesh shot off telegrammes to Bhagwan wanting to know the couple's whereabouts. The telegrammes were, however, intercepted by Babuji, and Bhagwan never received them.

When there was no news still for almost six months, a worried Kamlesh went to New Delhi. There, Babuji's mistress-cum-public relations woman told her she could not meet Bhagwan or Babuji. When Kamlesh pleaded with her, saying that all she wanted was news about her sister, she was told that no one except Bhagwan or Babuji knew where they were.

Deeply suspicious by now, Kamlesh went to a local gurdwara and sought help from the priests. Initially, there was some hesitation on their part as they didn't want to rub the powerful Bhagwan the wrong way. Besides, in matters where religious sentiments were involved it was difficult to get police cooperation unless one had some evidence. The only facts at hand were that Pappi and Sanjay had gotten married and that they were now missing. But they agreed to go to the local police station where a friendly police inspector listened to their complaint.

The inspector had a grouse against Babuji. The long and short of it was that Babuji had once threatened the inspector following an altercation between an ashram driver and a beat constable. The driver was arrested and taken to the thana but had to be released the moment Babuji landed up with a mob of followers and hangers-on and began to throw the names of the Prime Minister and senior police officers around. The inspector was abused, pushed around and told in no uncertain terms that his job was on the line if he did not release the driver. The inspector had neither forgotten nor forgiven Babuji for the insults heaped on him. This was as good a time as any to get his own back.

But when they reached the ashram gates they were not allowed inside by the security guards posted there. There was only one way out and that was to get a court order, so Kamlesh moved the courts. The magistrate listened to the case and ordered the ashram to produce the missing couple. Babuji saw the order and realised it was something that had to be complied with. There was no point in risking the wrath of the court and if Babuji was frightened of anyone or anything it was the legal system. He had too many skeletons in his cupboard to take on the judiciary.

He agreed to let Kamlesh in but warned her that Pappi had lost her mind and wasn't herself. When she accompanied the inspector into Babuji's house, she was taken to a small, unlit room where Pappi sat cowering in a corner. There were bruises on her face from repeated blows to it, her hair had not been combed for days and she had no clothes on. The inspector was dumbstruck and Kamlesh fainted at the pitiable sight of her sister. A sheet was hastily procured and Pappi wrapped up in it and brought out. Kamlesh recovered enough to help her on with some clothes and without further delay Pappi was taken out of the ashram and into a nursing home.

The doctor who examined her noticed that Pappi had been badly beaten up all over. Since she was too traumatised to speak no one knew what had happened to her. She was given a sedative and Kamlesh put her in a taxi and drove with her immediately to Mansuri. The doctor had prescribed some medicines and advised complete rest. A heartbroken Kamlesh did the next best thing she could. She wrapped her sister and herself up in the dark and safe cocoon of Cliff Hall, and began to nurse Pappi back to what she hoped would be a semblance of normality.

FOURTEEN

Many days passed, Pappi lying motionless in bed all the while. Then, one morning, Kamlesh heard Pappi call out to her. The two sisters clung to each other as Pappi let loose a long long-dammed torrent of tears and in between managed to find her voice. Soon she was able to eat some porridge and as she sat in the feeble light of a wintry sun in the back of the house, she thought it was time to write all about her experience. She told Kamlesh about it and the elder sister agreed it was a good idea for her to pour out her troubles on paper. She had discussed the matter on the phone with a doctor in New Delhi and he too thought it would be good therapy. Kamlesh was convinced that there was nothing wrong with Pappi and the whole story about her insanity had been cooked up by Babuji. The diary or the account of her short-lived and tragic marriage was passed on to me and here are the extracts from it.

(I have taken certain liberties with what Pappi wrote because most of it was illegible and sometimes one had to interpolate. I have also censored some of the more disgusting accounts of the sexual indulgences of the people involved, in the cause of good taste.)

Pappi's diary:

I suppose my wedding was not all that spectacular because Bhagwan did not want any ostentation. Kamlesh had decked me out in my mother's jewellery that had been taken out after many years in the bank, polished and made to look new. It was antique stuff and worth many times its weight. The diamond pendant alone was worth a few lakh and the old-fashioned earrings with long strands of gold that went around my ears were also studded with priceless diamonds and other stones. The bracelets made of solid gold were too heavy for my slender wrists and I was only able to wear them for the wedding as my arms felt tired if I wore them for too long. On my feet were golden anklets and diamond toerings made of huge diamonds.

It was the kind of jewellery that people from the old days—like my mother—had inherited from their mothers and they from theirs and so on, over the years.

The 'nath'—the nosering—sported a diamond so heavy that I took it off immediately after the ceremony for fear that my nostril would tear. And all my fingers had rings on them made of diamonds and emeralds, rubies and pearls. These, alas, had to be left behind in the ashram when Kamlesh came and took me away.

We went on a honeymoon and initially, I wasn't too worried about the lack of sexual ardour on Sanjay's part. I was itching to make love but he kept putting it off from day to day with one excuse or the other till I thought it wiser to enjoy the sights and food of Europe, and leave it at that. At least once a week I wrote a postcard to Kamlesh and kept her abreast of my travels. But I didn't mention the lack of physical intimacy because I felt too embarrassed. As a matter of fact, I had worried about it even in the days when we were courting. Sanjay was a proper and conservative man and I would console myself by saying that things would be different once we were married.

Initially, I thought that there was something wrong with me. The smell of my body perhaps, or some such thing, which turned Sanjay off. I changed my hair oil, wore some of the expensive perfumes I had picked up in Paris, but none of that seemed to make any difference. He was polite and gentle but whenever I wanted to embrace him to arouse him, he would turn his back to me and mumble something or the other which was signal enough that he didn't desire me. I kept my disappointment to myself mainly because there was no one to confide in while we were travelling. My blouses became more daring as I showed more bosom than was necessary. I had large breasts and used to be the envy of most of the girls I knew in school and elsewhere. In our room I would wear the sheerest of negligees and made every attempt to expose as much flesh as was dignified. But nothing seemed to work and so I resigned myself to the thought that maybe he would respond once we got back to India and to the more familiar comforts of his house.

However, a rude awakening awaited me. In New Delhi we had our rooms above Babuji's. The idea was that we would have the privacy to come and go as we pleased. At least that was what I was told. But it was only a day after we were in New Delhi when I inadvertently walked into the ground floor bedroom of Babuji to find him and Sanjay in bed and fondling each other. I stared at them for what seemed like an eternity and then with the realisation that the two were lovers I ran to the bathroom where I vomited. All this time Babuji's mistress, who he said was the public relations officer for the ashram, lay alongside them and fondled both of them. Needless to say, all three of them were stark naked.

I think there comes a time in a woman's life when she feels worthless and unwanted. Here was the man who I loved who could only be aroused by Babuji while my so-called valuable assets went ignored. What further sickened me was that the ménage à trois took place right under my nose and I couldn't think what to do about it. I suppose my sounds of disgust had taken the three out of their sensual unconsciousness because I was seen. Soon after, Sanjay entered our bedroom and sat down next to me where I lay face down on my bed weeping at my ill fortune.

I told him I wanted to leave him because I found the situation intolerable. It was all so strange to me and there was no way I was going to put up with his sexual preferences. I had got over my initial shock and now I was losing my temper. I think I shouted at him, called him names and told him I would report the matter to Bhagwan.

He begged me to keep quiet. He told me he would make me rich beyond my dreams and that I would be free to lead my life as I wished. Even if I took on a lover he wouldn't oppose it. All he wanted was to keep the marriage together in the eyes of the world. After all, Bhagwan's son couldn't in any way be seen to be flawed. It would destroy the very basis of his existence, he told me.

In my excited state I didn't hear half the things he said. But I do remember him telling me how Babuji used to sodomise him as a child, and how later, when he returned from England, the relationship continued because Babuji controlled the purse-strings. He could only live the life he led if he agreed to do what Babuji wanted him to do. Which meant sleeping with him and that obnoxious woman who was also his mistress. He said everything changed after he met me, but it was too late, he had lost the desire for straight sex and the only way he could find pleasure in the sexual act was with another man and with a woman's anus. When Babuji wasn't around, he added, he often went to male prostitutes. But he couldn't expose himself in public because he was vulnerable to blackmail, and hence the need to maintain this whole business of being happily married. No one, least of all Bhagwan, suspected his homosexuality and he begged me to forgive him and keep his secret.

I was now in two minds. I initially wanted to leave him forever. I felt humiliated and wasted in that sort of a situation. But then I reasoned that maybe there was a cure for his malady and perhaps I could, over time, seduce him like some ancient apsara and conceive his child. Fatherhood might bring about a change both physical and mental and with this fond hope I agreed to stay with him.

Nothing significant happened in the next few days and we were leading a life that passed for normal in public. We would give audience along with Bhagwan from the balcony of his apartment. But deep in my stomach I had that hollow feeling that my life was doomed and my youth would be wasted.

I knew Moni Baba and I would often catch him looking at me in a knowing way. I was afraid he had caught on or maybe was adept at reading people's minds. I couldn't confide in him for fear that Sanjay would lose his position and be thrown out of the ashram and disinherited. There were worse things that could happen to him because I had heard that Moni Baba was also a tantric and could cast a spell on anyone. So, I had to be careful of him and that was what Babuji had also told me in rather menacing tones.

My life was centred around my small apartment, the daily drive to Bhagwan's apartment dressed in all my finery, and the dreaded prospect of spending sleepless nights, unloved and unwanted. Many a time I thought I would write to Kamlesh and tell her about the situation at the ashram. But then I hesitated because I wondered what her reaction would be.

Perhaps she would lose her temper and blame me for what had happened. After all, I had led her to believe that Sanjay and I were in love. Would there be a repeat of what had happened between me and Kukku? Would I have to make Kamlesh share my ignominy? I loved her too much to make her go through the same emotional disruption all over again.

While these and other morbid thoughts crossed my mind I found I had lost my appetite for food. I would nibble at whatever came up from the kitchen and leave the rest. If Sanjay noticed he didn't say anything. As a matter of routine, we hardly exchanged any words except for curt good mornings. Within ten days of our return from Europe, he had taken to sleeping in Babuji's room and I was left alone and abandoned.

I realised I was a prisoner. I again wanted to write to Kamlesh but could find no paper nor a pen. It struck me then that everything had been deliberately removed.

I searched the apartment but to no avail. When I tried to go downstairs I found the door locked. Suddenly, I became too aware of my surroundings. I shook the mist that was covering my mind like a dark blanket and began to knock furiously on the door. Nobody responded. When the woman who brought me my lunch came, she opened the door with her key and locked it immediately after her. She never spoke and never smiled once. I realised that she was deaf and dumb. When I signalled for a pen and paper she looked blankly at me and gestured that I should eat. When I didn't and threw the thali at her, she calmly picked up the silver utensils and, after cleaning the mess on the floor, left the room, locking the door behind her.

Then began a period of no food or water. For a day or two I put up with that form of punishment. Punishment it was because when I complained to Sanjay all he said was that that was what I deserved for being so difficult and short-tempered. He called me a spoilt bitch and said if I didn't like life at the ashram I could go back to my 'damned' sister. I didn't know why he was calling my sister names. At that point in time I didn't know that Kamlesh had tried to enter the ashram but was turned away.

I had been without food or water for days when Babuji came to my apartment and, catching me by my hair, dragged me to a small, dark room at the back of the house. There he kicked me and beat me up, and in my weakened condition there was nothing I could do. Then he tore off my clothes and left me there cowering in my nakedness. *(She also mentions some of the unspeakable, sexual things done to her by Babuji at length. But as I have said earlier I have censored it.)* There was no sign of Sanjay nor of Bhagwan. Nobody wanted to know what was happening to me. I tried shouting for help a few times but I was too weak to make any noise. Then I lost consciousness and it was only when Kamlesh and the police inspector broke down the door that I realised that help was at hand.

There is something else which puzzled me no end. It was the persona of Moni Baba. Surely, if he could read my mind, he would know what was going on in the ashram. I think he knew all about Babuji and his dirty bag of tricks. But he didn't do anything about it. If it was true that he was a tantric then why wasn't he punishing Babuji? Couldn't he cast a spell on him?

FIFTEEN

The moment Pappi recovered her wits and had more or less got over her trauma, Kamlesh decided to move court for a divorce. The marriage was dead and there was no question of even trying to revive it. Not with Sanjay's proclivities and the viciousness of Babuji. What Kamlesh feared the most was some kind of revenge from Babuji's henchmen. Babuji himself had been restrained by a court order but then court orders didn't mean much to trained assassins. There was nothing to stop them from killing both the sisters. The other more important thing was that Kamlesh wanted her family jewels back in her possession.

Extracts from Babuji's diary. (This diary was recovered by the police in later raids on the ashram and produced in court as evidence against him. I have translated from the court records as the diary was written in Hindi.)

In the ashram, Bhagwan and Moni Baba had been whisked away on a lecture tour on my orders so there was no one asking for Pappi or Sanjay. At any rate I had spread the word that the two had gone on another honeymoon and wouldn't be back for a couple of months. I had accompanied them just to make sure that no word reached the top men. I knew that there were informers who would plant stories in Bhagwan's head and damage my control over the activities in the ashram.

Of particular interest was the deaf and dumb woman who used to serve food to Pappi. She had been witness to the raid by the police and the forcible snatching of Pappi from right under my nose. I knew that she could spell trouble for me because I sensed that she didn't approve of my actions, specially the starvation and beating up of Pappi. I did like her pert arse though. Besides, she had seen me sodomising Pappi on many occasions. I had brought her into the ashram after I had found her raped and abandoned by the roadside near a village I was passing through on one of my innumerable journeys. I knew I could keep her close to me without fear of being betrayed. She was my personal servant and as such had access at all times to my apartment and, by association, could have been privy to many or most of my secrets. But since she was deaf and dumb I had little fear of her. Besides, she knew no one besides me and who was she going to tell, anyway, and who would believe her? She was just a castaway.

Now, things were different. The woman had seen the police come in and I knew that much of my hold on her had been diminished. In her eyes I was as vulnerable as any other human being. And that, from my point of view, wasn't a good thing at all. I gave the matter some thought while on my travels and eventually rang up my trusted assistant to get rid of her. The man made the necessary arrangement by asking two of the goons that were fed and clothed by me to take the woman to the banks of the Jamuna and drown her.

The goons caught hold of the woman just before she was going to sleep. They knocked her out cold and, after wrapping her in a sheet, carried her to the banks of the river. The mistake they made was that the place where they took her was full of weeds, and the river, during the lean period, didn't have much water in it. They first raped her and then dumped her there in the hope that she would eventually drown and her body would float up like so many bodies did on the Jamuna on a regular basis, and nobody would be wiser. After all a woman was murdered or raped or both every few minutes, according to some statistics. It was a time-tested method and the two thugs lost no time in getting drunk in the small town around the ashram.

End of excerpt from diary.

~

From other accounts this writer gathered in his research, the woman, after being thrown into the water, didn't sink as the murderers had planned. Her sari acted as a life belt as she slowly drifted down the river. The reeds also helped to keep her afloat, and when she regained consciousness, she had no problem in standing up and walking ashore. Because it was night and very dark she didn't know where she was so she kept walking along the bank, downstream and away from the ashram.

When dawn broke she stood on the bank shivering and pondering on what to do. Nothing looked familiar to her and she decided to keep walking to keep warm. After a while the sun came up but in the winter haze it hardly gave her any warmth. A breeze had also picked up and she felt colder than she had in the night. She left the bank and began to move inland along what was a well-used path. Soon she saw a village and smoke rising from cooking fires.

Some children saw her as she walked down the main kuchcha road on either side of what was the village. They began to follow her. One of the bolder boys threw a stone at her but when she made no sound the children thought she was some kind of a ghost and ran away screaming. An old woman poked her head out of her hut and saw her. Sensing her plight she beckoned the woman inside and made her sit by the fire. In the smoke-filled room the deaf woman saw that the old woman was obviously alone. There weren't many utensils around except the bare essentials. The old woman was a widow and childless and like many Hindu widows, had been shunted out of the centre of the village to its periphery.

The widow had nothing much to offer her except a thin gruel made of dal and rice. She offered some to the woman who took it greedily and drank it down in one go. Somewhat restored, the deaf woman then signalled that she was deaf and dumb. The old woman nodded and told her to sleep for a while because she had to go and make her morning rounds begging for food. While her family had abandoned her after her husband died there were still some in the village who were compassionate and took pity on her plight. So she begged for her sustenance and somehow kept body and soul together.

The deaf woman slept in fits and starts and woke up when she relived in her nightmare the rape and beatings by the two thugs. Such is the helplessness of handicapped people that they think nothing of such hardships. She had landed up in the ashram because of another similar incident and had quite gotten used to the idea of getting physically violated and abused. She sat in a corner waiting for the old widow to come back.

—⁂—

SIXTEEN

Many years ago, when Moni Baba jumped off the Vivekananda Bridge into the Hooghly, he had been temporarily deranged because of certain incidents in his life. Those happenings had made it unbearable for him to live anymore, or so he thought at the time. Over the years he had resumed some form of sanity and the yogic exercises and meditation in the high Himalayas had restored his memory to quite an extent. He now knew who he was and after considerable thought allowed his new identity of Moni Baba to take over. He had forgotten and rejected the world of Calcutta. Immersed in his new life, he hung on to the young Sudip Biswas who progressed from a young yogi to a guru and became the man known as Bhagwan. After having been together for almost fifteen years, Moni Baba had decided to take Swami into confidence by telling him that he could speak, read and write but chose to stay the way he was (appeared) because he didn't want to attract any attention to himself. The Bhagwan respected his wishes and the two of them, while together, were still many miles apart in some ways.

Life in the ashram had given Moni Baba the minimum comfort and total anonymity needed by a man with a past and he was quite satisfied with the way life had spun out for him. He was a copious reader and in the privacy of their room would talk to Bhagwan about many things both spiritual and worldly. In that sense he was a far more enlightened man than Bhagwan. His talks eventually became the discourses for which Bhagwan had become famous. Bhagwan had the necessary attributes to be a leader of people. These, in the main, were his good looks and baritone voice. He was only too grateful for Moni Baba's help. Somewhat like a parrot and armed with a prodigious memory, he could recite almost ad verbatim all that Moni Baba told him. It was what is known as a good working relationship.

Moni Baba had also begun to keep a diary soon after they had set up the ashram in Allahabad. In this book, which he always kept next to him whether awake or asleep, he noted down his thoughts and observations of the life around him. It was what is known as a 'khata' the red cloth-covered book used by banias to keep their accounts. It had come into my possession by a strange quirk of fate (that I will talk about later) and will help to a large extent in knowing what transpired in the ashram and later in

Mansuri. From time to time I will quote extensively from it because it is the one authentic source of the story I am telling you. Here again, I have taken liberties because his account is a mix of Bengali and English and is more coherent when put out in simple English.

Moni Baba's notes:

The day I jumped off the Vivekananda Bridge on the Hooghly near Calcutta I was certainly not in my senses. A few hours before I decided to end my life I had killed my wife who I thought was unfaithful to me. Like most suspicious, jealous and erectile-dysfunctional husbands I thought she was sleeping with other men, particularly my business partner, Sita Ram. My partner was from Marwar in Rajasthan and I was from an old Bengali family.

But I had no proof of a relationship and so had kept the suspicions to myself. The business was started by my grandfather and we were manufacturing various kinds of ayurvedic remedies for some of the most common problems faced by people. Malaria was a recurring problem created by the British—it was believed. In their plans to modernise India, the colonisers had laid down railway lines and built bridges which blocked large sections of free-flowing water. The stagnant water was the favourite breeding-ground of the anopheles mosquito that is the carrier for the disease. It is the most debilitating of all fevers and a man or a woman with malaria was bound to, in those days, die a slow death from the disease.

If I remember right, Sita Ram's father used to be a munshi with my grandfather and later my father. Sita Ram joined the business when I needed cash to expand and modernise our marketing. Since we had almost grown up together he was the natural choice for a partner. He also seemed to have the necessary money though I found out much later how his father had accumulated it.

Life in Calcutta was one long round of parties after parties. We flitted from one club to the other, restaurant to restaurant, bar to bar. Most of us were having affairs with each other's wives and if we were not, we certainly lusted for them. It was the life of the idle rich and had been handed down to us by our fathers who, like most of the nouveau riche, lived ostentatiously. Their spending money was made by evading income tax and other taxes which they should have paid as good citizens. But they didn't. The reasoning was quite simple. It was our wealth and we had the freedom to spend it any way we wanted to. Besides, they needed black money to bribe the hundreds of palms held out by inspectors— labour, excise, tax, police and so on. Then they needed the extra money to keep the leaders of the unions happy so that while they could make all the noise they wanted, they would not sabotage production or the sales of their products.

No one bothered to react to the growing number of refugees from the east—East Pakistan, now Bangladesh. People flocked to the city in thousands and for want of better places to stay, camped in the open and on pavements of the city's grand streets. Slumlords made a killing. From the City of Palaces, Calcutta began to disintegrate into a City of Slums. Some French writer called it the City of Joy but it was well established among the city's thinking people—and there was no end of them—that the city was doomed to extreme poverty and it was only a question of time before the people on the streets united and burnt and looted the palaces of the rich. There were a lot of false alarms like the Naxalites; disillusioned communists who united under the banner of Maoist-Leninists. They thought, like Mao, that power came from the barrel of the gun. They were no longer interested in parliamentary democracy, which they saw only as a decadent political system in which the rich became richer and the poor poorer. In a sense, that was what was happening all over the country.

I was more than an interested spectator in the happenings around me because of my association with all kinds of people from all walks of life. I knew sportsmen, writers, filmmakers and sundry intellectuals and we met on a regular basis at the

Coffee House on Central Avenue. The coffee soothed my hangovers and the talk acted as a salve to my disturbed conscience. But I was too far gone into decadence to worry about such niceties. The 'addabazi', as these gossip sessions were known as, was a good enough arena to vent our spleen on imagined and not-so-imagined crimes by the State, the capitalists (I was one of them), the workers (most of us were not) and the general decline in morals and other standards of life. That was in the Coffee House. Outside, garbage gathered on street corners because the Corporation was not able to get work out of its sanitation workers—the vast majority of whom were 'ghost' employees. They existed only on paper and their salaries were collected by canny babus.

Riots, demonstrations and violence were a way of life for many. The decadent lifestyle of my set was also one way of life. It never ceased to amaze me how the movers and shakers of the city went around like sleepwalkers. They seemed to be intoxicated by the power of money and rarely bothered to worry about the creeping breakdown in most civic facilities, electricity and other essential pleasures of city life. If there was no power they had generators. There was no shortage of cheap servants and it was quite common for the city's well-to-do to have several servants. From time to time you would see gross display of money as the richer merchants fed thousands in the memory of their dead mothers or fathers. Or on the marriages and funerals that were celebrations, whichever way you liked. There were also people like Mother Teresa who looked after the dying and talked about a compassionate God and love. But by and large these were sentiments that were ignored because everyone seemed to be busy in the pursuit of material well-being.

I knew many husbands who overlooked their wives' infidelity for one reason or the other but mainly because they were up to the same thing. In my case the matter became doubly difficult to digest. First, my money was being appropriated without a care in the world. I had worked hard for a business degree in the US and wanted to put my ideas into practice. Most of them were working out but for the manipulation of the books by my partner Sita Ram. I remonstrated with him and possibly not strongly enough because he fobbed me off with one explanation or the other. Most times he would stay away from the plant because he said he didn't like to breathe in the fumes and dust. He worked from my house and he worked on my wife at the same time.

I wouldn't have known about him because I trusted him implicitly—although I had reservations about his money-management techniques. But then I had the attitude most people seemed to have. It was 'What the heck!' So what if Sita Ram was salting away money? So long as I had enough to live it up, pay my club bills, run my fancy vintage car, and keep my wife in the style she was used to. Her style required regular visits abroad for shopping expeditions as neither my wife nor I were inclined to wear Indian clothes or shoes or jewellery.

And then I had my old ayah who had been my childhood nurse and of whom I was rather fond. One day she came to me and with tears in her eyes told me that the mistress had sacked her. I asked her what for and initially she kept quiet and wouldn't answer me. Slowly I coaxed an answer out of her and learnt that she had caught my wife and Sita Ram in flagrante delicto. When I confronted my wife she said so what? She also told me that I was lousy in bed and showed no real affection for her. Also, I didn't give her parents the respect due to them. And that I had kicked out her brother from my company. I didn't tell her why I had sacked the thieving and slimy character. Her false accusations were a bit too much. I strangled her. And she died. Possibly, she had it coming over the years. She had a barren womb and lesser men would have kicked her out of the house a long time ago. But I too had my weakness.

I then marched into Sita Ram's office on the ground floor and did the same to him. I squeezed his scrawny neck so hard that I felt a vein burst somewhere in his head. And that was that. I can't recollect exactly what happened after that except that I was standing in the middle of the Vivekananda Bridge and looking down at the dark and swirling water of the Hooghly. I climbed to the top of the guardrail, took off my gold watch and gold necklace, placed my wallet on the railing and jumped off. I don't think anyone saw me jump and if someone did he must have made off with my watch and wallet. All that I remember after that is meeting two young men who took me under their care, and we drifted around till we reached the mountains.

There, in the cave where we lived with our guru, I learnt to come to terms with my conscience. I also learnt to let bygones be bygones and that there was no way of ever going back to the past. Our guru told us to live day to day and our karma would take care of the rest. Over the years we mastered many yoga ashans. We learned to control our breathing, about kundalini, and I was instructed in various tantric rituals.

Somewhere along the line my voice came back to me and my hearing became normal. But I didn't let anybody know and it was only after we had left the cave and set up our own ashram under the guidance of Bhagwan that I confided in him. He was initially surprised but when I began to share my thoughts with him in total privacy he began to respect me and told me so. He also asked me to take care of some aspects of administration when he learnt of my earlier life and because he didn't fully trust Babuji. I did that and began keeping an eye on the accounting methods of Babuji. Sure enough, the man was fiddling with the books and I wasn't too surprised at his greed and crookedness. After all, when you've lived with a man like Sita Ram, you do learn a trick or two. By then my memory had more or less been restored and I knew that in my Calcutta incarnation I was a man called Somdeb Banerjee.

⸺⟨ø/ø/ø⟩⸺

SEVENTEEN

Excerpts from Babuji's diary:

A time was coming in my affairs when it seemed prudent to beat a hasty exit to nowhere land. The murder of the deaf and dumb woman was simply another happening but the rescue of Sanjay's wife by her sister was another business. I knew that they would file for divorce and a lot of dirt was going to come out of it. I didn't think I had anything to say in my defence and I doubted if Sanjay could say anything either. What Bhagwan would do when the scandal made it to local newspapers was anybody's guess but my goose was cooked for sure.

The divorce papers landed on my desk by registered post and I immediately called a high-powered lawyer I knew who was also a devotee. One good thing about running an ashram is that a whole lot of powerful people—bureaucrats, lawyers, doctors and politicians—come and anchor their directionless ships at Bhagwan's feet. Businessmen are no different because they have so many secrets that their consciences need the daily dose of a sermon to keep them dead. And Bhagwan's sermons were a particularly effective palliative for troubled consciences. I didn't have any scruples about what I was doing and so my conscience was clean as a whistle. I didn't need any sweet pills. So long as nobody found out the real me, I was simply Bhagwan's trusted man, God-fearing and totally devoted to furthering the ashram's goals of bringing mental peace to the whole world. Besides, I reasoned, if people can bribe stone statues of various gods and goddesses from Tirupati to Badrinath, what was wrong with me, a mere flesh-and-bone mortal at that, taking my commissions from the overflowing coffers of Bhagwan? He himself could be said to be taking some consideration for his sermons. Wasn't he?

The lawyer, a corpulent, corrupt and vulture-like man in his black robes, greeted me on the steps of the High Court when I went to see him. He escorted me to his chambers and asked how he could be of use. I told him about the divorce papers. The papers mentioned the grounds of divorce as 'irrevocable differences'. Fortunately, there was no talk of mental and physical cruelty nor of Sanjay's homosexuality. But somewhere along the line I knew the subject would crop up because the judge was bound to ask why the differences had come about. Then there were the witnesses, specially the police officer who was an unimpeachable witness. But we could say that he had been suborned or maybe he would turn hostile if I paid him enough. The deaf and dumb woman had been taken care of and I had my public relations bimbo who could counter the witnesses from Pappi's side. The doctor who treated her could be taken care of and all in all it looked quite good for us.

The only thing the sisters wanted was Pappi's jewellery back and that was going to be a bit dicey as I had had the stones taken out and the gold melted. Of course, they would have a tough time furnishing proof of ownership as the jewellery was quite old and had not been registered. I could also plead that Pappi was insane and that she had been married under false pretenses to Sanjay and that her sister had hatched the entire plot with an eye on the boy's fortune. They could be shown as plotting and devious women because I had enough devotees of unimpeachable credibility, including former judges of the Supreme Court, who could be made to testify on our behalf. I told all this to the lawyer who agreed and began to draft a reply to the charges made against us.

The case came up for hearing in Mansuri as the marriage had been registered there. My lawyer marched in with a smart retinue of juniors, and devotees in the hundreds gathered outside and inside the court. Across from us sat the two sisters and their lawyer, a portly gentleman who looked half asleep. I had had him investigated and learnt that he was the top criminal lawyer in the district if not the state. I was also told that he was a hard drinker but totally incorruptible. But then, most small-town lawyers could be bought or intimidated and I was confident I would be able to turn the tables on him when the time came.

My regular goons were also in attendance and looked quite menacing as they escorted Sanjay to the court. They were armed with spears and guns and I was sure they could strike the fear of God in anyone who dared to confront them. Bhagwan did not know anything about the court case but I wasn't too sure about Moni Baba who had been giving me rather hard looks of late. Neither of them were in attendance as they were not required.

The judge took his seat and the court proceedings began. I sensed immediately that the local lawyer was more important than he looked. In my experience most of these lawyers who hang around the courts looking half asleep are actually wolves in sheep's clothing waiting to pounce on the unwary and vulnerable. Behind their sleepy looks and lazy demeanour they have razor-sharp wit, and more than make up for lack of fine legal knowledge by sharp and sometimes questionable courtroom tactics, including bullying witnesses. I was wary of him and didn't have the faintest idea as to what his plan or strategy was. I don't think my lawyer did either despite his deep knowledge of the law.

The judge immediately set a date fifteen days from that day to hear the lawyers. The entire matter was being heard in public and that was because this was in the days before divorce proceedings began to be held *in camera*. It was obvious that the sisters' lawyer's will had prevailed because all this meant that we had to return to New Delhi and turn up again. My lawyer started to say something but the judge brusquely told him off and announced the next case.

We filed out of the courtroom silently as there was little to be said. Outside, the devotees led by my goons began to shout slogans against the judge which was a bad move because the opposite lawyer immediately drew the court's attention and the next thing was that we were told to clear out of the premises. When we reached the more public area of the Mall, some of my goons fired in the air as if to celebrate but in actual fact, to intimidate the sisters and their lawyer.

Before they knew what was happening the police came and arrested them. It was again obvious that the sisters' lawyer had primed the police and they were waiting for our side to break the law. All the men bearing arms were arrested, their arms seized, and they were marched off to the nearby police station where they were booked and, within an hour, taken away to the district headquarters where they were denied bail and sent into police custody. I was later told that the police beat them mercilessly and made sure that they stayed inside under various infringements of the law. We had lost the first round.

That evening we held a meeting to figure out what to do. These were happenings we weren't prepared for. Things seemed to turn from bad to worse when, the next day, the local press openly turned against Bhagwan and his devotees. We were branded as hoodlums masquerading as religious people. The very reporters who had been friends with us till then because of the largesse I bequeathed to them every time we came to Mansuri, were now our foes. Not a good omen. We could do without any publicity, leave alone bad stuff. What made it worse was that even the devotees who did not know of the case and had not come to Mansuri for the trial, were informed of it by the newspapers in their home towns. Nothing more devastating than bad press, I can tell you. The devotees, in turn, sent telegrammes inquiring about what had happened.

The news was also read by Bhagwan and Moni Baba in New Delhi. The dreaded phone call came early in the morning and though I had an explanation I wasn't prepared for the cold fury in Bhagwan's voice. He wanted to know why he wasn't informed about the goings-on in the ashram and all the business about Pappi being rescued. I told him in my usual lying way that Pappi had gone mad and was throwing violent tantrums. Because I was afraid that she might hurt herself I asked the sister to come and take her back to Mansuri. I had arranged for the police, another untruth, to escort the sisters back to a nursing home and that explained their presence. I told him that I had to do all this because Sanjay was mentally very disturbed by the turn of events and had left the country and gone off to England. Another lie. For the time being, Bhagwan was mollified. But only for the time being.

<hr>

EIGHTEEN

Excerpts from Moni Baba's diary:

This morning I saw Bhagwan angry for the first time. He was very disturbed by the news reports which were brought to his attention by yours truly. He read them in utter disbelief and immediately asked to be connected to Babuji in Mansuri. On the phone he asked him why he was being kept in the dark and when Babuji told him that Pappi had gone mad and he had to take some action, otherwise Sanjay could get hurt, Bhagwan cooled down a bit.

In the privacy of our chambers we discussed the matter. I was convinced that there was much more to what Babuji was telling us and I suggested to Bhagwan that the public relations woman be summoned and interviewed. Generally, no one was allowed in our private chambers but this time we had to keep things very quiet and so we made an exception. The woman came and prostrated herself at Bhagwan's feet. He told her to get up and I think it was the first time the woman saw us at such close quarters. It was eyeball to eyeball and Bhagwan told her in no uncertain terms that she better come up with the truth.

She was quaking at the knees and looking at our grim countenances, she was on the verge of tears. It was obvious that she had a lot of things to hide. I think she was deciding in her mind which way to go. If she was disloyal to Babuji then she was doomed for certain but if she stayed in Bhagwan's good books she was relatively safe. I saw that she had come to a decision and began to talk. In the beginning she was hesitant but as she warmed up to her confession it all came out in one big cascade of words.

She began at the beginning and told us that she had been married to a well-known film actor in Bombay. At the outset, life had been a bed of roses but soon things began to sour as the man would bring in different women all the time and make love to them in her presence. She was forced to watch and if she didn't he would thrash her mercilessly. She wasn't allowed to leave the house and was in reality a prisoner at all times. The few times he took her out was to big parties where he would hold her tightly and wouldn't let her out of his sight for a second. She tried to run away and one day succeeded and made her way to the Victoria Terminus and caught the first train leaving for New Delhi.

In the train she met Babuji who, after hearing her story, told her that she could come and live with him in the ashram and help out with his work. He agreed to pay her enough money to keep her in good clothes and she began to live with him. Soon they were lovers and she was very happy with the way things were going for her. She felt, she said, safe and was momentarily quite happy. But then Sanjay returned from England and things began to change.

At this point she hesitated and stopped. Bhagwan prompted her to go on and with a great show of disgust and repulsion she told us that Sanjay and Babuji were lovers and she was forced to make love to both of them. At this point she broke down and beseeched us to look after her as her life was in great danger. When asked why, she told them about how Babuji used to beat Pappi up and had her locked naked in a small room and kept her on a starvation diet. She also told us about how Babuji had ordered the murder of a deaf and dumb serving woman because she was a witness to the events in his house and that the thugs hired by him had dumped her in the Jamuna.

We were astonished, to say the least. This was one side of Babuji's personality that we had no idea of. I had my reservations about him but as far as murder, violence and his homosexuality were concerned we had never even thought about it. Bhagwan was getting red under his collar and I could see flashes of anger in his eyes. He was very near to losing his self-control and I terminated the meeting with a wave of dismissal. The woman rose to her feet and backed out of the room as it was considered rank bad manners to show your back to Bhagwan.

Once she was gone and the door closed behind her we pondered on what we had just heard. That there were orgies going on right under our nose was bad enough for the reputation of Bhagwan and the ashram. Now his son was found to be a closet homosexual and his daughter-in-law had been literally driven out of the house. Bhagwan felt that we should do something concrete before the word spread. As it was the newspaper publicity of the divorce proceedings had made a terrible dent in Bhagwan's standing among his devotees. Now if the other sordid secrets ever got out we were ruined for sure.

End of excerpt.

---***---

NINETEEN

Dr Jadu Ram Mishra and Satya Prasad Kala were out for their regular evening walk when they ran into Ram Prasad Maithani, Kamlesh and Pappi's lawyer. Satya Prasad and Ram Prasad had been classmates and were friends, in a manner of speaking. They were two different personalities—the teacher a pedantic sort and the lawyer a flamboyant 'hail fellow, well-met' sort of chap. Since they had known each other over a long period of time there weren't too many secrets between them.

Maithani told them that he was off to a local bar and they could join him for a coffee. The good doctor excused himself as he had no wish to hang around a bar but Satya Prasad took up the invitation as he had no problems with anyone drinking though he himself was a teetotaller. Once they were comfortably seated they began with small talk about each other's families. Then some gossip about mutual acquaintances and finally they got down to the case.

Satya Prasad introduced the topic by asking how the case was progressing. Maithani smiled and said, 'Just as one would expect it to. The bastards are lying through their teeth and we are going to nail them. You know, a lot of people think we lawyers are the crooks. But these holy-shmoley wallahs are the ones to look out for. I tell you, if I had my way I would wring that bugger Babuji's neck.'

'Why would you do that?' Satya Prasad asked.

'Why would I? Because the son of a bitch is one mean man. You know what Pappi and Kamlesh have told me? I'll tell you because it is going to come out in the trial anyway. He is a pervert and a sadist, with both men and woman, and so is Pappi's husband. That poor Pappi has been shattered by that marriage. If you go through her diary, you'll understand the hell she had to go through in that ashram,' Maithani said.

Satya Prasad raised his eyebrows in shock. 'I always suspect there is something wrong with all these godmen. God only knows how many people are fooled by these sorts every day. If I had my way I would line these good-for-nothings against a wall and shoot them,' Satya Prasad said disgustedly.

'Yes. So would I. But there is a law in this land and it must take its course,' Maithani said.

'Surely there should be a law against such charlatans? They are perpetuating a fraud on all of us, aren't they?' Satya Prasad persisted.

Maithani laughed and said, 'You know, that American showman Barnum is credited—wrongly, as history tells us—for saying that a sucker is born every minute. In our country there is no shortage of those people who want to meet God by proxy. You must see the following these so-called godmen have. Thousands and thousands of people, mostly poor and gullible, line up to listen to their piffle. The rich, on the other hand—and I can tell you with some authority as a criminal lawyer—need to put some kind of a salve on their conscience. Chances are that they have committed some kind of crime or the other on their way to becoming rich. These godmen come in handy for them.'

The two men talked about this and that and Maithani promised to keep Satya Prasad abreast of matters as they developed. But he reiterated his intention to nail Babuji and the others one way or the other. He said he was looking for a witness who could come and testify in court. The only eyewitness Pappi had told him about was a deaf and dumb woman but she had disappeared from the ashram shortly after Pappi's rescue. There was the police inspector but Maithani said he could never be sure of policemen as they were so easily corruptible. And he didn't want a hostile witness. As far as Kamlesh was concerned, she could easily be branded a prejudiced party by the opposition lawyers. All the same, he would ask her to testify though she could have a tough time during cross-examination. The men parted and promised to meet again.

TWENTY

The deaf and dumb woman, after her close brush with death and the rape, had recovered sufficiently to tell her host, the old widow, that she could read and write. After staying in the woman's hut for a few weeks, she found work as a servant in the village landlord's house. It was there that she read about the divorce case in the local paper. She asked her mistress where Mansuri was and she was told that it was far away and up in the hills. Her entire communication was done by writing out her questions and the landlady would in turn write down her answers. By and by, she (the afflicted woman) said her name was Janaki and she only remembered a few things from her past. For instance, she didn't know where she had come from. When asked how she knew how to read and write she said she couldn't remember but must have had had an education of sorts.

The landlord was a decent kind of man and was also active in local politics. Since they weren't too far from New Delhi, he was a regular visitor to his party's headquarters. On the way there, before crossing the Jamuna, he used to pass Bhagwan's ashram. He never bothered to pay much attention to it because he was fundamentally a socialist. He didn't believe in gurus and bhagwans who he thought were first-class crooks and freeloaders.

Janaki had told the landlord's wife that she had lived in an ashram once and it was from there that she had been kidnapped, raped, beaten senseless and thrown into the Jamuna by two men.

His wife related this to the landlord and the man was intrigued enough to make discreet inquiries about the ashram from the local police station. There he met the inspector who had helped to rescue Pappi. The inspector told him that the ashram was run by one Babuji, who was a total fraud and a crook. The Bhagwan was a learned man but he had very little to do with the day-to-day running of the ashram. As such he had no idea about the corruption and venality that the man called Babuji had let loose in his name. The only problem, the inspector said, was that he couldn't get enough evidence to put Babuji behind bars. But he was biding his time and was sure that the man would slip up some day.

When the landlord told him about Janaki and what she had to say, the inspector was elated. He said he would like her to go to Mansuri and testify in court. As a matter of fact, he would like to take her personally since he was bound to be called up to give evidence one day or the other. The landlord said he would only be too pleased to be of any help.

But when he left the police station he had doubts

about the inspector's integrity. He had some idea about how the police worked and he knew that many of them were not to be trusted without circumspection. What was to stop this man from betraying the deaf and dumb woman? Suppose Babuji and his people came up to him with an offer he couldn't refuse? What would be the chances of him selling off Janaki? The landlord wasn't quite prepared to trust the man completely.

Instead he took the unusual step of leaving his village and going to Mansuri. He had never been to the hill station before and like many before him he was mesmerised by its beauty. Since he didn't know anyone there he went to the police station and asked about the case. He was told that the case was being conducted by one Maithani and he could meet the lawyer for more details. Maithani had his chambers in the town and the landlord went there. When he told Maithani the story of Janaki—how she was thrown into the Jamuna to drown, but by the grace of God managed to survive and land up in his village—Maithani was simply overjoyed. He now had the case sewn up and with Janaki as a witness, he knew he would get his man.

He asked the landlord where he was staying in town but the landlord said that he was planning to go back to his village as he had not brought any warm clothes. Maithani insisted he stay the night in his house and, reluctantly, the landlord agreed. That night—as Janaki's landlord sat in a borrowed shawl—they talked more about the case and it was agreed that the landlord would bring Janaki whenever the lawyer asked him to.

The next day the man went back to his village where he told Janaki about his meeting with the lawyer and that she would be required to testify in court. Janaki signalled she would most happily testify because she had seen that poor woman being brutalised by Babuji. Besides, that man and his henchmen had attempted to kill Janaki herself.

In Mansuri, Maithani told the sisters that by a strange turn of events a man had come to him and told him about Janaki, a deaf and dumb woman who was an important witness in the case and was willing to come forward to testify. Kamlesh was thrilled to hear the good news and now she was convinced that they would send Babuji to the gallows for sure.

The case came up for hearing on the next date but the Delhi lawyer asked for another. The judge said that he would allow him an adjournment but warned him that he wouldn't brook any further delaying tactics. Maithani wanted Babuji's passport impounded by the court and an assurance that Babuji and Sanjay would be available at the new date. The Delhi lawyer agreed.

TWENTY-ONE

Excerpts from Moni Baba's diary:

The meeting with Babuji's public relations woman, who said her name was Kamla, had for the first time yielded some firm evidence of Babuji's chicanery. Bhagwan had instructed Kamla to keep him abreast of all that transpired and it was Kamla who came and told us that the court had demanded Babuji's and Sanjay's presence at the next hearing. Swamiji and I discussed the matter and thought it best to write to the magistrate and make it clear that we were not a part of the conspiracy against Pappi, but now that we knew some of the facts, we wanted both Babuji and Sanjay punished under the law.

Kamla had also told us about how Babuji had the valuable, and antique jewellery that Pappi brought with her as her dowry, melted and the stones taken out of their settings. These, she told us, were now kept in a bank locker but she didn't know which bank. We had decided to return every single item that belonged to Pappi. Since we could not save the marriage because of Sanjay's deviance we had come to terms with the fact that a divorce would be in the best interest of all concerned. Swamiji wanted to disinherit Sanjay and ask him to leave the ashram.

Of course, he was willing to give him some money to survive but he wanted to have nothing to do with him anymore. However, there was his mother and I told him we should consider her happiness too as she was the innocent party in the whole affair. The matter was postponed for the time being and Swamiji said he would think some more about it before taking action.

Kamla had been told to provide us with a list of all the banks where Babuji kept his money and also the name of the Swiss bankers. We told her to wheedle the information out of him by hook or by crook. Otherwise, Swamiji told her in an ominous voice, Moni Baba would cast a tantric spell on her. Kamla was one frightened woman after that. I don't think she would have been frightened of the law or any other man but a tantric spell was something that would bring ruin upon her and possibly turn her into a leper or something worse. Of course, I wouldn't ever think of doing anything like that—not that I knew how to go about it. It was just one of the myths about me and my tantric powers. But in this case the very threat of it worked.

I don't know how she managed it but she got the names of some of the banks where Babuji kept his loot. She told us that the money was kept there in the name of a trust purportedly headed by Bhagwan and that it was believed Babuji operated it with a power of attorney. This was news to us.

Bhagwan said he couldn't remember signing anything remotely like a power of attorney. Yes, he had signed some papers some time ago about a trust but couldn't remember the details because he hadn't bothered to read the document. He had left it to Babuji as he had left all business matters in his hands ever since he came to the ashram almost thirty years ago. Babuji was then a relatively young man, may be in his early thirties, and he had told us that he had worked for the government but now he wanted to work for Bhagwan. We had believed him then, and though I had my doubts, I had never voiced them. Now that we knew better, it was time to take some action to salvage whatever we could before the matter became public.

I suggested to Bhagwan to summon Babuji and ask him to show us the trust document. Also, that all the banks named by Kamla be notified that Bhagwan had withdrawn all powers of attorney from Babuji and that the latter was not entitled to deposit into or withdraw from any account of the ashram. I thought that for the time being this would suffice. Bhagwan, who rarely used the telephone except to talk to special disciples, rang up the banks concerned and advised the bank managers accordingly. He also asked them take a new specimen of his signature. The banks complied and it was a good thing for us because we were able to save some of the funds of the ashram before Babuji shifted them elsewhere.

When Babuji came to see us, Bhagwan asked him to show us the power of attorney. Babuji said it was in his office and he would bring it immediately. He left and did not return till late in the evening. I saw the document and signalling him to leave it with us, dismissed him. I read through the document and saw that it was an outright forgery. Everything had been faked including Bhagwan's signature. The man had assigned powers to himself that had in effect made Bhagwan of no account. I thought it was high time to report the matter to the police.

———◦◦◦———

TWENTY-TWO

In Mansuri, Maithani had an early morning meeting with Kamlesh and Pappi before setting off to the court. It was decided that if Babuji and Sanjay did not show up Maithani would ask the judge to issue non-bailable warrants to them along with instructions to the authorities to seize the ashram property.

The time had been set for the first hour, and still, there was no sign of the two men. After a reasonable wait Maithani moved an application for issuing non-bailable warrants and seizure of the ashram property. He also produced Janaki in court who signed an affidavit in front of the judge detailing the happenings in the ashram beginning with the beating and locking up of Pappi, denial of food and fresh air, stripping her of all her clothes and the rest of the sorry story.

Then came the bombshell when, in another statement she accused Babuji of attempting to murder her and having had her thrown into the Jamuna by two of his thugs, whom she also named. In passing she mentioned that the two men had also raped her.

This woke the judge up and, calling Maithani aside, he said that the matter had assumed very serious proportions and he had no choice but to order Babuji's arrest. It couldn't have been better for Maithani who now had Babuji where he wanted him. Sanjay was small fry because he was only party to the divorce proceedings, but rape and murder were a different matter and Babuji was up to his neck in the conspiracy.

The judge's order prompted the police to send a party to New Delhi to arrest Babuji. But the man had disappeared and when they entered the ashram they were taken by Kamla straight to Bhagwan. The police confronted him and Moni Baba with the complaint by Janaki and a shocked Bhagwan just shook his head and cursed Babuji under his breath. There wasn't much he could do by way of helping the police because he had no idea of where Babuji could have gone. As far as Sanjay was concerned he would summon him back from England immediately, he told the police.

Faced with no clue as to the whereabouts of Babuji, the police team returned to Mansuri. But while in New Delhi they called on the police station near the ashram where they met the inspector who had helped in Pappi's rescue. When he was told about the attempted murder by Babuji and his henchmen, the inspector promised to do all in his power to trace the missing man.

He began his search by interrogating the driver of Babuji's imported Mercedes. Initially, the man said he had driven Babuji to the airport from where he had boarded a flight but he didn't know where to. After a little persuasion and threats of seizing his driving licence, the man admitted that Babuji had flown to Bombay. The inspector warned him to not leave the ashram till further notice and went looking for Kamla who, till that time, was supposed to be a confidant of Babuji. She could only give him the names and addresses of some devotees in Bombay where Babuji had stayed in the past.

With something to go on, the inspector went to his superiors and got permission to follow the trail to Bombay. The biggest problem was that he did not have a name for Babuji. He was simply Babuji and nobody seemed to know any other name he might be operating under.

The inspector knew that a lot of people joined

ashrams to lose their identity and it was quite clear that Babuji and his assistant were among that kind. The same applied to the thousands of swamis and babas who dotted the landscape. It was like looking for a needle in an upside-down haystack.

At the airport he scrutinised the passenger manifests for the flights that had left for Bombay in the days after Babuji disappeared from the ashram. He was looking for a name to the face and when a helpful check-in clerk identified the fat man in the photograph he was shown to the inspector as one P.P. Sharma, the inspector thought he had hit the jackpot.

⸻ ❧❧❧ ⸻

TWENTY-THREE

Excerpts from Babuji's diary:

My meeting with Bhagwan and Moni Baba told me that my game was up. I had to make a run for it. I guessed that it was Kamla who had spilled the beans on me and it was a matter I would look into at some other time. I mean, I had given that woman a life after her disastrous marriage and now she had betrayed me!

I was in Bombay and had checked into the Sun-n-Sand, a fancy hotel much in favour with filmmakers who often shot their poolside scenes there.

I had shed my ashram clothes and was dressed smartly in a deep blue safari suit. My beard and long hair had disappeared and I looked to all intents and purposes a successful businessman, and those who saw me lounging around the poolside bar must have figured me out to be a big-time producer. I had called my lawyer in New Delhi once and he had given me more bad news. I learnt that the deaf and dumb Janaki, who I presumed dead, was alive and had submitted a statement in the court where she had accused me of attempted murder. I was also told that a warrant had been issued for my arrest and that the police were hunting for me.

In my experience it does no good to surrender to the cops. It is best to let them arrest you. The reason is very simple. They have to prosecute and need to have enough material to make the charges stick. Nine times out of ten they do a shoddy job of it and most criminals get away scot-free.

In the meantime I was enjoying the various pleasures Bombay had to offer. I had put out that I was interested in bank-rolling a film, and a number of hopeful writers and directors had turned up with story ideas and scripts. I wasn't quite interested in the scripts because I was told by someone in the know that the Bombay film world worked differently to the way I'd thought. The main thing was to sign up a star cast. The leading man should be a young and upcoming star and so should the leading lady. Then there were assorted side-roles with enough young men and women vying to act in them.

I went a step further and hired a secretary, and instructed him to rope in as many stars as he could. I also got a writer to do a script for me in which all these superstars would have roles, and some others would do cameos. I wanted it to be an action film with lots of fights, car chases and the usual romantic angle. Songs were a necessary part of the formula and it was decided to have at least twelve songs so that each hero and heroine got a song sequence. The rest I left to a director while I bought myself a TV and a video player and watched tapes of successful Hindi films the whole day.

By the end of a week I had more or less figured out the secret of a film's success. I told the director of my discovery who, like all the chamchas in Bombay, agreed wholeheartedly. We had to have beautiful sets and a lot of razzmatazz and some shots had to be shot abroad, preferably in Switzerland and England as most audiences were familiar with the locales there.

Work started in right earnest. The leading stars were signed on and soon the first of the dance sequences was shot. I would leave my hotel to visit the studio and the sets from time to time. But I generally stayed in the background and avoided the press like the devil. The story line was simple. The plot centred around a gang of professional thieves and a determined police inspector out to catch them before they brought off the biggest robbery in India's history. It was working out quite well and the director assured me that we had a superhit on our hands. My job was to bankroll the project and I did that in the initial stages. After the first few dance sequences had been shot, we screened them for distributors from all over India and they liked what they saw. Soon I had huge advances for various territories, and the film was guaranteed a successful run.

The first inkling I had that the police were hot on my trail was when the hotel manager, who had become a friend as I was a long staying guest who paid regularly and tipped handsomely, told me that someone had been around, asking questions. I asked him if he knew that someone. The manager said he didn't but he could show me the man. The man was sitting in one corner of the pool, sipping a cold drink and was wearing dark glasses. Even from a distance I could make out it was the same police inspector who had come to rescue Pappi with Kamlesh. I pretended I didn't know him and told the manager that he might be a prospective writer or an out-of-work actor.

I didn't waste much time. I had always kept an open ticket and visa for Dubai in my wallet, and in no time was on my way to the airport to board the next available flight. However, what I didn't know was that the Bombay Police too had been alerted about me and I was arrested as I was about to check in. They handed me over to the inspector who had come from Delhi and the next evening we were on a train heading north. Because I was willing to pay the fare we were travelling in air-conditioned first class and the journey was progressing quite comfortably. The young policeman told me his name was Satpal Yadav and he was a jat from western UP. I tried to engage him in conversation but he simply smiled and said he had nothing to talk about.

The night passed and the next morning we were pulling into New Delhi station where a small posse of policemen was waiting for us. I was bundled into a jeep and driven off to the police station near the ashram. I had already been told about the charges against me and was also informed that I would be handed over to the Mansuri police to be tried for attempted murder. I was allowed to contact my lawyer and soon saw him dragging his corpulent self into the station. He had a chat with the inspector who said we would have to wait till the Mansuri police got there and it might take the whole day. I was kept in custody and, at lunch, offered some simple food. The Mansuri police arrived later in the evening and it was decided that if I paid for a taxi we could leave for Mansuri immediately. The other option was to go by the night bus and I was in no mood to travel by bus. So a taxi was ordered and I was bundled into it with two policemen riding on either side. I was also handcuffed just in case I got any ideas of escaping.

Escape was the last thing on my mind. I knew that there was little point in even thinking of that. I wouldn't have got very far even if I bribed the police. So I went meekly and pretended all the time that I was an innocent man who had been roped in for all the wrong reasons and that I was obviously a victim of a deep-seated conspiracy. The policemen seemed bored by my account and the senior inspector who had come from Mansuri told me to shut up and save my breath for the judge.

We reached Mansuri early in the morning. The police gave me some tea and biscuits and, around ten, I was produced in court. The judge read the chargesheet, looked at me and heard Pappi's lawyer mumble something about setting a date for further hearing. In the meantime, I was sent off to the district jail in the valley. My lawyer didn't say a word because there was nothing he could say at this stage. And soon I found myself in jail where I was given a corner in a barrack along with some really hardened criminals. However, my lawyer arranged for my stay to be as comfortable as possible and money was put in the right hands. Later in the day I was moved to the jail hospital where I was given a bed and clean sheets and blankets. It was here that I waited out my days before my trial started.

❦

TWENTY-FOUR

Maithani and Satya Prasad Kala were sitting in Maithani's office and Maithani was rather excited by the developments.

He told Kala, 'The police got that bastard Babuji. Now we have him in jail and I'll make sure he stays there. He's going around by a different name, P.P. Sharma. Apparently it is his real name and we have asked the government department he had worked in for some details of the charges against him that had led to his dismissal.'

'That's good news,' Kala said. 'What about the boy Sanjay?'

'Oh, him? He's not important. He's just a party to the divorce. He'll be divorced and Pappi can do whatever she likes. It's that man Babuji. He needs to be punished. Wait and see how the can of worms will open now. I bet that Bhagwan fellow will have something to tell the court when I have him summoned,' Maithani said.

'Like what?' Kala asked.

'I don't know but I can guess. Men like Babuji have a lot of skeletons in their cupboards. While working for the government, he was thrown out for embezzlement and soon after disappeared into the ashram. There is no way a mongrel's tail can be straightened. Ashram or no ashram. He is bound to have continued with his criminal habits. We'll know soon,' he said and smiled.

Kala said he had to go for his walk with Dr Mishra and left Maithani's office. When he and the doctor met up on the Mall, Kala briefed him on what Maithani had told him. He told him that Babuji had planned to murder a servant who was a witness to the torture inflicted on Pappi but the woman had survived and was giving testimony against him. There was no way he was going to get out of that one, Kala said.

'Are you sure? You know judges can be bribed. At least that is what the public says,' Dr Mishra said.

'Yes, maybe. But all judges are not corrupt. Besides, Maithani is a tough and competent lawyer and I don't think any judge is going to go against him. At least not in this district,' Kala said.

'I have heard that the defence often buys up the prosecution. What are the chances of Maithani selling out?' the doctor asked.

Satya Prasad dismissed the suggestion offhand. 'Inconceivable,' he said.

The two men continued their walk, and their talk turned to the politics of the day, which was a favourite subject with the doctor. He had fixed views on politicians who he felt should be whipped every morning. He would often quote some Chinese philosopher who was supposed to have said that all children should be slapped twice a day. When a disciple asked him why, the philosopher said the first time in the morning would be to make sure he wouldn't do anything wrong during the day, and the second time when he came home just in case he had. He had a low opinion of all politicians and considered Nehru a hypocrite—a view Kala did not subscribe to. They would often argue about the merits of various men and women leaders and could never agree on them. But it kept them from getting bored and their friendship continued on an even keel.

On the way they passed Cliff Hall, which, from the outside, looked abandoned. The sisters had closed all the windows and heavy drapes shut out all light and peeping toms. If one did not know better, one would assume that the owners were not home. But they were, very much, and in their morning meeting with Maithani had been told of Babuji's arrest. They discussed this development and Pappi felt a cold shiver run down her back at the very mention of Babuji's name. That he was in jail was no consolation to either of them because they knew they would have to face him in court and the very thought frightened them.

Dr Mishra glanced towards the cottage and said, 'It must be tough on the sisters. All alone and nobody to talk to.'

'Yes,' said Kala and added that they had their gods

who would surely bring them solace.

'That may be. But the last Bhagwan they trusted has done them dirty. I doubt if they will ever go near these so-called holy men anymore,' the doctor said.

'I do hope they don't. This must be a telling lesson. Pappi has been traumatised by this incident and Kamlesh too has been scarred,' Kala said.

Soon they had come to the end of their walk, and with promises to meet the next day at the usual time, parted company.

As twilight advanced to dusk and dusk to night, a man could be observed standing outside Cliff Hall. He seemed to be watching the house. He stood motionless for quite a while in the shadow cast by the street light. Kamlesh peeked through a chink in the drapes and saw him. She had been seeing him ever since the court case started. He would come at a fixed time and stand there motionless, looking at the house. Then, the man would glance at his wristwatch and walk away. He was usually dressed in an overcoat and hat and a thick muffler covered part of his face. Kamlesh had told Maithani about this mysterious figure and he had joked that it was some secret admirer. Kamlesh wasn't too sure but, strangely enough, felt no fear. It seemed to her he was like some kind of guardian angel watching over them, and she thanked the gods for sending him.

Banoo, the eunuch, too, didn't miss this observer. He made him into a love-struck fan and, as far his cronies and certain townsfolk were concerned, that was the gospel truth. The way Banoo told his story, the man was actually the ghost of some Englishman. And, as he told his avid listeners, all ghosts of Englishmen were great fornicators. The rest he left to the imagination of his audience.

———◦◦◦———

TWENTY-FIVE

In jail, Babuji was visited by Sanjay. The young man came because he had returned to India to face trial on the instructions of Bhagwan. But he still needed to be guided by Babuji because he was entirely dependent on that one man who had done everything to corrupt him physically and mentally. All that fancy education was wasted on him as he couldn't think for himself. He was a weak kind of a man who stammered when in difficulty. Babuji was the crutch he needed to get on with his life. One thing he was sure of was that he wasn't going to go to jail for anything.

He looked around and wrinkled his nose in distaste at the surroundings. Everything smelt of urine and human excreta and he held a perfumed handkerchief to his nose. He would turn against Babuji and testify against him, he promised himself.

When Babuji came out of his cell to the area where he was allowed to meet visitors, Sanjay didn't recognise him for a moment. The man was clean-shaven and wearing a smart safari suit, highly polished shoes and smoking an expensive cigarette.

'So, Sanjay you have finally come,' Babuji remarked and waved him to a bench.

Next to them were women waiting to meet their husbands, mothers to see their sons and lawyers to meet their clients.

'How are they treating you?' Sanjay asked with a tremble in his voice. He had heard stories about how prisoners were beaten up, sodomised and tortured with chilli powder up their arses. He was scared of a life in jail.

'Couldn't be better,' Babuji said with an oily smile.

'Anything I can bring for you?' Sanjay said.

Babuji laughed heartily and said he was well looked after and was not in the barracks with the other prisoners but had a bed to himself in the jail hospital.

'Everything is for sale here and if you have the right kind of money you can live like a prince,' Babuji told him.

Looking at the man, Sanjay believed him. The man was obviously in good health, sounded cheerful enough and actually seemed to be enjoying his confinement. His greasy face shone with good living, his Colgate smile never wavered for a moment and his teeth glistened white. Sanjay wondered, however, what was going on in that crafty mind. The caste mark on his forehead had disappeared along with the beard and long hair. He looked what he claimed he was—a film producer. And there was a film being shot in Bombay to prove his credentials. He told Sanjay that he was now P.P. Sharma, and that when Sanjay was asked to identify him in court he must say that he didn't know him.

Sanjay knew what those instructions meant. If he didn't do exactly what Sharma told him to do he was in for some very big trouble. He feared for his life because he was aware of what Sharma had done to Janaki. What he didn't know was that Janaki was alive and had given an affidavit in the court accusing Babuji a.k.a. Sharma of having planned and commissioned her murder.

As Sanjay prepared to leave the obnoxious surroundings of the jail, Sharma again reminded him of what to say in court—and this time his eyes were as cold as those of a dead fish.

❦❦❦

TWENTY-SIX

Excerpts from Moni Baba's diary:

As soon as we heard of Babuji's disappearance and the subsequent court case, I realised that the matter could get out of hand. By then we knew that Babuji was an arch villain, the type who wouldn't hesitate to use every weapon within his reach—and that included murder—if necessary. I feared for the life of Pappi who I had grown quite fond of in my silent way. She was like the daughter I should have had. When I had expressed my disapproval of the marriage Bhagwan had joked my objections away by saying that I was just a jealous old man. I didn't think much of Sanjay to begin with. He did not have the robustness and joie de vivre of youth. Instead, he was pale, hollow-chested and gave the impression of being a man with no sense of purpose or ambition. He was also asthmatic, and Bhagwan would often explain away his listlessness and effete ways to his sickness. A good wife will do him a world of good, Bhagwan used to say. I always wondered what would happen to the unlucky woman who would marry him.

The marriage went through anyway and I felt sorry for Pappi. She seemed a sensible kind of woman and I assumed she was aware of the various proclivities of men. As things turned out, she was traumatised when she saw the real face of her husband. Sanjay had indeed played dirty by agreeing to the marriage, and my suspicion, quite rightly as we learnt, was that he had done it at the instigation of Babuji.

As far as Bhagwan was concerned, he had done Pappi a great favour by allowing her to marry his only son and heir. She would live like a princess, or so he thought. That fairy tale exploded into bits when the police went to the ashram to rescue Pappi and we learnt of the sordid goings-on at Babuji's house.

So one day I asked Bhagwan to give me some money because I wanted to go to Mansuri on my own and without attracting any attention. I feared for Pappi and her sister. He unhesitatingly laid out a large sum of money at my disposal along with some cheques on his bank account in Mansuri. I left the ashram one night without any one seeing me. I had had my beard shaved and hair trimmed. I had purchased a dark suit and tie for the first time in more than fifty years. I also rented a car and driver and pushed off to Mansuri where I checked into Roselynn Hotel that was run by a Sindhi couple. I told the owner, Prem, that I would stay at his hotel for a longish while as I was working on a book. He offered me an excellent room facing east when I asked for it.

The real reason for my wanting that was because from such a room I had a clear view of Cliff Hall and could keep an eye on who came and went. The girls only came out when they had to go to court. They were escorted by their lawyer and a tough-looking young man who, I learnt after making some discreet inquiries from the neighbourhood chowkidar, was a childhood friend. Apparently, this young man had some influence and muscle in the town. Provisions for the house were ordered by phone from the local greengrocer, their old family lala.

I also began to visit the courthouse, or kutchery, everytime a date was set, and followed the proceedings with keen interest. Their lawyer, a portly man called Maithani, was very skilled in a devious way. He never seemed to ask direct questions but invariably got the answers he wanted from the witnesses. On the other side, the lawyer from Delhi, waffled a lot and didn't get to the point, which rather upset the magistrate. He kept reminding the lawyer that the court's time was precious.

The divorce proceedings had been overtaken by the murder charge against Babuji who was now known as P.P. Sharma which, the court was told, was his real name. Maithani proceeded in his usual meandering way and established that Sharma was the man known as Babuji during his time in the ashram. He also told the court that Sharma had been dismissed from government service for embezzlement and had wormed his way into the ashram and Bhagwan's good books. He produced a long list of monies at Sharma's command which, Maithani told the court, Sharma had appropriated from the ashram's account. Further, he brought into court some of the contractors who were involved in building the ashram and made them testify to the fact that they had paid kickbacks to Sharma.

The even more enjoyable part of the proceedings was when Maithani introduced some women, who he said were prostitutes, and their madam. The women told the court that they were part of the brothel run by Sharma and had worked at the many melas he regularly organised. A lot of Babuji's supporters were seen slinking out of court and outside, the crowd thinned perceptibly. Sharma's lawyer was getting red under his starched white collar and the judge was smirking.

When the prostitutes were deposing, both Pappi and Kamlesh sat with their mouths agape and in obvious shock at the revelation. The Delhi lawyer didn't have anything to say except to object a few times, and after a while, he simply walked out of the court. His juniors, when their turn came for cross-examination, were the laughing-stock of the people gathered in the court. I had the feeling that the crowd was brought in by Maithani. Often, the prostitutes spoke rather explicitly, which embarrassed the lawyers. Eventually, the judge seemed to have had enough and adjourned the court to the next day.

TWENTY-SEVEN

In the town, people following the case were in two minds. Those who stood to gain from Bhagwan's largesse defended him stoutly. Their argument was quite simple: great men don't always know what their minions are up to. This theory was pooh-poohed by the others who felt that the eventual responsibility lay with the head of the ashram—and that was Bhagwan. They called him a fraud and local newspapers talked of barring him from the district.

All this information reached Bhagwan through Moni Baba who often sat with his host Prem and discussed the day's developments. Prem, an educated and sophisticated man, had no time or patience with swamis of any kind. He would most often dismiss Moni Baba's queries with a laugh and excuse himself to go off on some errand or the other. But the hotel waiters had all the gossip which they promptly shared with Moni Baba. It never crossed their rather simple minds to question Moni Baba's interest in the matter. They regarded him just as they would any other hotel guest who was also a generous tipper.

Moni Baba also saw the young, tough-looking man who escorted the sisters to the court come to the hotel quite often to sit around with Prem. The two men were engrossed in some discussion or the other and paid no attention to the elderly man sitting in one corner of the lounge reading a book or the newspapers. One day, he heard the young man tell Prem about the proclivities of Babuji and Sanjay. He called them 'queers' and they both laughed. For a while they talked about homosexuals in general which, Moni Baba noted in his diary, was nothing strange because many men found homosexuals objects of derision. Not only that, Moni Baba wrote, they forgot that some of history's greatest men were gay and made no secret of it.

The street lights came on and Moni Baba put on his hat and overcoat and went down to the Mall from where he had a clearer view of Cliff Hall, and took up his usual position in the shadows. He had been there for a couple of hours when the young man who was sitting with Prem walked by him, then turned around and stopped. The two men looked at each other and nodded in recognition. Nothing was said and the young man walked away.

From Cliff Hall, Kamlesh looked through a gap in the curtains and saw the man in the overcoat and hat standing there at his usual position. She heaved a sigh of relief and after putting off the lights, went to her bedroom. On the street, the man slowly began his walk back to the hotel. A dog barked somewhere, the late-night show at the Majestic Cinema ended and a thin trickle of people poured out and hurried homewards. It was just another night in Mansuri by the time Moni Baba went to sleep.

~

In the jail in the district headquarters, Babuji, now known as P.P. Sharma, tossed and turned in his bed in the hospital. He had been given a meal brought from the best restaurant in town, and after smoking a couple of imported cigarettes he took a turn around the ward and then lay back to sleep. But his world of dreams deserted him. Instead, he had a repeat of a nightmare that had been haunting him of late. In the nightmare he would see the face of Janaki but it was also the face of an avenging Kali, red tongue hanging out, blood dripping from the scimitar in her hand and a garland of human skulls around her neck. He would see himself being trampled underfoot and would often wake up bathed in sweat, and screaming.

The prisoners were quite used to such behaviour from other inmates. After all, there were quite a few of them in there on charges of heinous crimes like murder, burning brides and raping and killing children. The doctors would give the ones with severe problems of conscience some sedatives and forget about them. They did the same for Babuji but even then, he slept fitfully and never woke up fresh and cheerful as was his wont.

In all probability Babuji did not have a conscience.

But the thought of hanging from one end of a rope is good enough to induce the fear of God in many a hardened soul. One would have to be totally senile not to fear the gallows, and whatever people said about Babuji, no one would call the man senile. When awake, his mind was highly alert and he was forever plotting and planning. His lawyer would drop in often and they would chalk out a strategy but the case looked hopeless. They would jointly curse Kamlesh and Pappi for having brought all their troubles to such a head. And Babuji cursed the two thugs he had ordered to get rid of Janaki for their ineptitude.

The lawyer had been told to get someone to bribe all the witnesses. When the lawyer said he wasn't having much success with that, Babuji told him to meet a thug he knew in Varanasi who would murder Janaki for a couple of lakhs. That was more easily said than done. Janaki now enjoyed police protection round-the-clock after Maithani told the judge that he feared for her life. In another related development the police had got hold of the two thugs who were supposed to have murdered Janaki. They had confessed to the rape and the murder and were now prime witnesses for the prosecution.

TWENTY-EIGHT

In his chambers the judge was writing out his judgment. He had heard the witnesses for the prosecution. Maithani had feared that they might turn hostile but, strangely enough, they didn't. The reason was not that they did not fear the wrath of Babuji. They feared the tantric powers of Moni Baba more. The word had been sent to them through Bhagwan that if they recanted or changed their statements and confessions in any way Moni Baba would put a terrible curse on them. The two thugs were petrified of the mystic powers of Moni Baba or at least the myth surrounding them. Such are simple minds.

P.P. Sharma was red with rage, at least as red as a brown man can get. His eyes betrayed his anger though his fixed smile never left his face. He was already making plans for revenge. His lawyer stood by helplessly knowing that he had lost the case. Janaki's testimony and the statements by the two thugs sealed the fate of Babuji. Now the only question that remained was the quantum of punishment.

Maithani sat in his corner and you could make out from his expression what he was thinking. It wasn't the first time he had sent someone to the gallows and in his mind he was very clear that people like Babuji deserved what they got. From time to time he would smile at the sisters who smiled nervously back.

Eventually, the judge read out the sentence in court. The two thugs and Babuji were guilty of attempted murder. As such they were sentenced to life imprisonment. That meant fourteen years under lock and key, with the chance of being let out earlier for good conduct. Often, life sentences were commuted to shorter periods.

The next part of the judgment dealt with the divorce, and the judge said that since both parties were not willing to make up, the marriage was terminated. Sanjay was told to return the family jewellery, and an alimony was fixed for perpetuity. Sanjay heaved a huge sigh of relief. He had talked to Bhagwan and been told that an honourable settlement should be made with Pappi for the good of all.

There was also something for Janaki. The judge deemed it fit to announce a compensation for Janaki. He told the lawyer that Bhagwan should re-employ her, pay her enough money so that she got the best medical treatment for her impaired hearing and speech, and a cash settlement which would take care of her for life. The lawyer had no choice but to agree.

The police led away Babuji and the two thugs to the district jail in a police van. Sanjay disappeared the moment the judge concluded his statement, presumably taking off for the plains. Various bystanders and supporters of Bhagwan drifted away and that was the last anyone heard of them.

Moni Baba was sitting at the back of the court and had heard the judgment. He felt happy for Pappi but this was not the time to meet her or her sister. He too melted away with the crowd and drove off to New Delhi.

Back at Cliff Hall the sisters and Maithani sat around a pot of tea and congratulated each other. The months of tension were over and they could now live in peace. Maithani had worked out with the opposition lawyers the system of re-payment to the two sisters and the lawyer had brought with him a bank draft which more or less covered the value of the jewellery that Pappi had taken with her as her dowry. The alimony fixed by the court would be paid to Pappi annually and a cheque for that amount was also handed over to her.

After all the loose ends had been tied up, Maithani excused himself and went off to the bar to loosen up. He was followed by his juniors and some local friends, and a celebration of sorts took place. War stories were told and re-told about the various cases the old lawyer had fought and won. Finally, when they had had enough, they wound their way home to sleep the liquor off.

~

Excerpts from Babuji's diary:

I had discussed the matter of appealing to the High Court with my lawyer. He felt it was pointless but said he would go through the motions anyway. After all, he was being paid—and well. He went through the motions all right, but the High Court rejected the appeal.

In prison, life was pretty smooth. Because I was educated, and had just crossed sixty, I was given preferential treatment. I should think so, considering what I was paying for it. One of the thugs, also in the same jail, was designated my personal servant, and he would fetch and carry for me. I spent most of my time reading and writing and working in the jail library. The jailor turned out to be a nice sort of a man who, while aware of my crime, seemed to ignore it. Perhaps because he was well looked after by me. I mean, when you have deposited a large sum of money in a man's account, you expect some privileges.

I had a cell to myself and because I was considered harmless, I could move around freely. I wrote and read letters for those prisoners who were illiterate. We would discuss their cases and I offered them legal advice. With the consent of the jailor I was allowed to conduct classes for some of the inmates. I taught them to read and write, which they took to quite well. That only reinforced my belief in the fact that given a chance, any human being can be as good as the best.

All this social work kept me busy during the day but at night, as I lay on my cement bed trying to get some sleep, I vowed revenge against everyone involved, especially that man called Bhagwan and his mentor, the Moni Baba. I had a special plan for Sanjay for his betrayal and, every night, as I planned and plotted, I dreamt of the various tortures I would inflict on him. Both Pappi and her sister figured in my plan too, but I had all the time in the world to work out my treatment of them once I got out of jail.

A long imprisonment is supposed to act as a deterrent to crime. I say 'supposed' because it wasn't doing anything of the sort for me. The days passed in relative luxury. I was able to reduce my weight considerably and didn't look like the corpulent Babuji that people knew in my days at the ashram. I read a lot and as you can see, I kept my diary up to date. There was no sense of remorse or regret which is generally associated with the concept of incarceration. All I wanted was to serve my term and get back to the world outside and carry out my plans of vengeance.

Since I am jotting down my thoughts I would like to say that my time in jail made me realise, more than ever, the power of money. It seems that every man has a price. My jailor and his staff were very nice to me. I could have anything I liked. When I felt like eating fish it would be sent for. The same applied to any other article of food that I wished for. From time to time I was sneaked out of the jail at night to see films. I could have escaped anytime but it would not have been a prudent thing to do. I was better off in jail and I was sure that people outside would forget about me soon enough. That suited my plans very well.

My servant massaged me every morning. A barber came and shaved me and clipped my hair when needed. The barber was also a prisoner who was interred for murdering the man who was having an affair with his wife. He too seemed to have no regrets. We would chat about this and that every morning and he became a sort of confidant and I became his. He told me the whole story of how he was betrayed by his wife for a man he trusted with all his heart. What had hurt him, he said, was his wife's attitude. If she hadn't been so blatant about of her affair with that man the chances were he wouldn't have bothered murdering the man. According to him he killed the man so that his wife would suffer the pangs of losing her prized possession. The barber wanted me to believe that he loved his wife too much to kill her. At the same time, however, he hated her so much that he wanted her to suffer for as long as she lived. Killing her would not have been the solution, he told me.

I suppose everyone has his or her logic for doing

what they do. I had mine when I ordered the murder of that Janaki. Mine was plain and simple greed to hang on to a life of extravagant luxury and pleasure. I knew at that point in time that Janaki was a stumbling block to my lifestyle and, as such, had to be done away with. I suppose the barber was right in his own way.

While the barber had had his revenge by killing his wife's paramour, I still had to have mine. I knew I had all the time in the world. My health was good and with any luck, and a bit of lobbying, I could get out of prison in a few years. At the least I would be only seventy, which isn't too bad a time in life—provided you are rich.

TWENTY-NINE

The furore raised by the case died down as suddenly as it had started. The doctor and Kala continued with their rounds of the Mall and while on one of those walks, the doctor said, 'Did you know that Bhagwan has stopped coming to Mansuri?'

'No,' said Kala. 'I couldn't care less anyway. The man had it coming. All these godmen are rogues, I tell you.'

'I have a postcard from an acquaintance who was

also a devotee of Bhagwan. The man says he must have stopped going to the ashram because no one seems to be living there. The gardens are in a bad state, and weeds and wild grass have taken over the once beautiful lawns. The dairy farm has stopped functioning and there is no management to be seen. Except for a chowkidar at the gates who says he doesn't know anything about the Bhagwan's whereabouts. All he knows is that his salary arrives on time by money order from an address in Calcutta.'

'What about Moni Baba, the deaf and dumb tantric?' Kala asked.

'No mention of him,' the doctor said.

'I suppose they ducked out of sight, what with all the negative publicity and the scandal. I bet they've disappeared into the hinterland somewhere. India is a big country—there are millions of places a man can disappear to, aren't there?' Kala said.

'I suppose you're right,' the doctor said.

They dropped the subject because it was of little interest to them. Kala asked the doctor about news of Kamlesh and Pappi.

'I haven't seen them in a while. But my wife told me they are back to running their shop. I suppose they're all right now,' the doctor said.

'I wonder if they'll ever get over the trauma and the nightmare of those days,' Kala said.

'The mind is very resilient and people do get over these things. Sure, there will be some psychological scars—and perhaps they will have lost faith in people in general—but they'll survive,' the doctor assured him.

'I wonder how that swine Babuji is doing in prison. Do you think he will be full of remorse when he comes out?' Kala asked.

'Maybe and then maybe not. Some people are beyond redemption, and I suspect Babuji is one of them. Remember, he had been chucked out of his government job for misappropriation of funds. Then he went on and did the same with Bhagwan. Why shouldn't Bhagwan have sued him?' the doctor said.

'That's a good question. I think Bhagwan didn't want to drag the matter on too far because a lot of his ashram's dirty linen would have been hung out to dry in front of the public. These ashrams and Bhagwans all have some sordid thing or the other to be secretive about. Besides, they have so much unaccounted wealth that if the income-taxwallahs ever thought about investigating them, I bet they would unearth one gold mine after the other,' the cynical Kala said.

'Talking about sordid things . . . Did you know that Bhagwan used to have a mistress?' the doctor asked.

'What? A mistress, did you say? Who?' said a surprised Kala.

'There was this woman called Behenji who lived with him and, from what I have heard, mothered that bastard Sanjay. But the word was that Sanjay was his nephew and so nobody suspected Bhagwan of doing anything wrong,' the doctor said with a smirk.

'Where do you pick up such gossip?' Kala asked.

'Oh, Kamlesh told me.'

'That's interesting. Any idea what happened to Behenji and Sanjay?' Kala said.

'As far as I know they too have disappeared. I'm sure Bhagwan paid them a lot of money to keep them quiet. You know what I suspect?'

'No. What?' Kala countered.

They had stopped for a breather and were leaning against the railing that bordered the khud-side of the Mall. Beyond them the valley stretched out for miles and, since it had rained in the plains, everything was crystal-clear.

The doctor mused, 'Isn't it fascinating that though nothing seems to change, everything does. I mean the view. Can't remember it being the same twice. There is always some difference in the light or visibility or the clouds or the mist. Even the trees change their foliage with every passing day.'

'Yes,' said Kala. 'Only the mountains remain, a solid reminder of their permanence. But we were talking about your suspicions. What are they?'

'Yes. As I was saying, I have always suspected that Moni Baba. I think he was the brain behind everything in that ashram. Bhagwan might have been good at delivering sermons and all that but the real thinking person was that Moni Baba,' the doctor said.

'What about Babuji? He looked more of the type.'

'No. No. Babuji was a cheap crook. He had cunning and a mean streak. But this Moni Baba seemed to be above all that. I wish I knew more about him,' the doctor sighed in frustration.

They came to the end of their walk, and parted with promises to meet the next day at the same place and same time.

THIRTY

Excerpts from Moni Baba's diary:

I returned from Mansuri quite satisfied with the way the trial had gone. I told Bhagwan that the sisters had been compensated for their loss and trauma. But money is never the cure for the kind of hurt Pappi had suffered. Bhagwan hoped that time would heal her wounds.

The facts disclosed at the trial had more or less finished off the ashram. Fewer and fewer devotees showed up for Bhagwan's sermons and, seeing the way things had gone for us, I suggested that we remove ourselves to the old cave in the Himalayas.

Bhagwan didn't quite fancy the idea. I think he had gone soft. The luxurious lifestyle had destroyed the ascetic in him and perhaps drained him of the pure energy required to be a swami. Possibly, the idea of being Bhagwan had also gone to his head. Sometimes, too much adulation can push the ego beyond the realms of the mystic. Our guru had always told us to sublimate our ego. But we hadn't done that. Instead, we had let it take over our daily actions.

To begin with, Bhagwan was no longer a brahmachari—he slept with Saraswati. That by itself was a denial of the basic tenet of being an ascetic. He had let his baser instincts take over and that, as our guru had told us, was not conducive to maintaining a higher spiritual plane. Perhaps the riches that had been amassed for him by the rogue Babuji had made him see the human being that he really was.

When I sat down to do the accounts I saw that the ashram, meaning Bhagwan, had upwards of several million rupees in cash, jewellery and gold in equal amounts. Besides, there was the real estate which I found out was worth another fortune. Then there were the expensive toys—the fleet of Rolls-Royces, the helicopter and a private Gulfstream jet. When looked at in its totality this accumulation of wealth was obscene. And this was only the parts that had been salvaged. We had no idea how much Babuji had salted away in his accounts abroad.

Bhagwan simply shrugged his shoulders and said

all that wealth was God's gift. I reminded him that it was not money earned by hard labour. To that he simply smiled. I noticed that there had been a substantive change in his attitude to life in general and to Sanjay in particular. It was also obvious that father and son had grown closer than ever before because they could be seen whispering and talking in hushed voices like conspirators.

I knew that the young man was desperate, after the fiasco of his marriage and the scandal that ensued. Somewhere along the line he convinced his father that it was best that they depart for foreign soil. I think Bhagwan quite liked the idea because in no time at all they were packed and ready. There was no advance notice or warning, and Bhagwan calmly told me one morning that he was leaving India for good. According to his exact words he was going on a 'tour of the world'.

He also told me that he was leaving some money, and the deaf and dumb Janaki to look after me in my old age. Sanjay had bought a house in Allahabad and I could go and live there till my death. Saraswati was not part of their plans. She had been given a small fortune and was told she could go and live in Mansuri in the cottage that was once the ashram's summer headquarters. The New Delhi ashram was to stay locked till Bhagwan came back from his 'world tour'.

—✦✦✦—

THIRTY-ONE

The dust had settled. Babuji was locked up for the next fourteen years along with his henchmen, Bhagwan and his bastard had disappeared to parts unknown, Moni Baba was reported to be between Calcutta and Allahabad, and Kamlesh and Pappi had more or less resumed their normal lives. They no longer walked in fear and were able to put their creative energies into their work.

Their interest in things spiritual continued with a long list of new gods joining the old ones in their little temple at home. There is no shortage of gods in India.

The sisters went to meet holy men in nearby Haridwar from time to time. They tried out Reiki, conferred with a disciple of Sri Sri Ram and heard all about the Art of Living. You could say that they were leading what was a perfectly normal life for them. They had one or two friends who called on them at the shop and were profferred coffee and biscuits. No one was invited to the house and no one was allowed inside. They kept no servants and after Boy ran way, they dropped the idea of keeping another pet.

The years rolled by and from time to time they heard of the death of some acquaintance or the other. They made the necessary condolence calls.

Once in a while they attended a local wedding or two. Venturing out of Mansuri was a total no-no and even if they had to go to Haridwar or Rishikesh they would go in the morning and return by nightfall. They had insulated themselves in the safety of the small hill town and seemed quite satisfied with their lifestyle.

Almost ten years after the trial Saraswati, or Behenji, along with Moni Baba's deaf and dumb maid Janaki, went to the Kumbh Mela in Allahabad. There, a bizarre incident happened which closely resembles Hindi movies.

Among the millions of people gathered there to bathe in the Ganga was a family which transpired to be that of the deaf and dumb woman whom they recognised as 'Sheila Devi'. The chance encounter reunited all of them. Sheila Devi had apparently been the wife of a fairly well-to-do merchant. Her husband had died in the years after her disappearance but she had left behind two grown-up sons who had since married and had children.

The boys took their mother to the tent where they were camping. Such was the joy of the meeting that Sheila Devi found her voice again, and her hearing. You can call it a miracle, or whatever you like, but that's the way it was. She wrote to Moni Baba about the amazing event and told him she was now going to live with her children.

Moni Baba noted all this in his diary. He also

mentioned that he missed her gentle care of his daily needs but he had by then kept another young servant who cooked and cleaned for him.

The diary goes on to relate all that was happening in Moni Baba's life. He had begun to go back to Calcutta where no one recognised him because he had discarded the robes of a sadhu and wore ordinary clothes. Besides, he was no longer the rotund, dissipated person of his younger years. On the only visit to his ancestral home, he spent some time looking at it from the outside and saw that it was in a dilapidated state. The red brick masonry was overrun by moss and peepul saplings had sprouted in the cracks in the wall and on the roof. The huge gate had rusted at the hinges and hung to one side like a drunk leaning against a wall for support. He noted all that and saw little point in going inside. In a fleeting thought he wondered who was looking after the property. That was all the interest he had in his old home.

It was during this visit to Calcutta that he ran into his old companion, the man who had befriended him many years ago, Shankar.

In the Bhowanipore area there is an old temple and near that is a guesthouse where people from the outlying areas come and stay. Moni Baba was staying there because the food was simple but good and the accommodation quite comfortable for an ascetic like him.

Shankar was staying in the room next to him. He was a full-fledged tantric by then, with the mandatory long and matted hair; the chillum brandished like a badge of honour; and surrounded by a small group of disciples. It was the reek of marijuana that had drawn Moni Baba's attention to the room and when he peeked in he saw and recognised Shankar immediately.

He walked into the room and Shankar gestured to him to take a seat in the circle of people around him. It was obvious that Shankar had not recognised the clean-shaven and well-dressed Moni Baba. He asked him what he could do for him. Moni Baba, now very articulate, said he would like to meet him alone. He was told to wait. After a while Shankar got up and gestured to Moni Baba to follow him into an adjacent room.

'Don't you recognise me?' Moni Baba asked Shankar.

'Should I?' Shankar riposted.

'I am your old friend, Moni Baba.'

Shankar looked at him steadily and then, slowly, recognition dawned. He put his hands on Moni Baba's shoulders and slowly drew him into a powerful hug.

'What happened since we last met?' he asked.

Moni Baba told him about how he had recovered his voice and no one except Bhagwan knew about it. The entire story of Bhagwan, his son, Babuji, the story of the two sisters and all that had transpired in the years they had not seen each other was narrated in some detail.

Shankar said that money was the root of all evil and he was particularly angry when he heard what had happened to the sisters. He vowed to punish Babuji.

In his diary Moni Baba wrote: 'Shankar cursed Babuji and called him all kinds of names. He said he would cast a spell on him that would destroy him. He went on like that for a while and then suddenly lapsed into silence. Then he closed his eyes and began to meditate.'

According to Moni Baba, Shankar felt he had known the sisters all his life although he had never seen them. While innocent people were duped by the many holy men dotting the landscape, he had never taken advantage of any of his followers and he had quite a few.

All they wanted was the comfort of his words, his attempts to solve their myriad problems, and in most cases he had succeeded. He never asked for anything—like money or fame—in return, and if he got some, he re-distributed it among his other followers. He was leading the life of a true ascetic.

Was his life all that perfect? Didn't his hashish-addled mind ever think of anything other than blessings or revenge? Can a human being be at the extremes of Love and Hate at the same time? Possibly. The mythical Shiva was supposed to be like that. He too could create and destroy. So, what was to prevent his ardent and fanatic followers from taking to the same line of thought? Shankar was his namesake and as namesakes go, he was duty-bound to follow the Master.

THIRTY-TWO

The lifeline in small towns is gossip, some malicious, some harmless but mostly useless. Speculation about the weather, people and prices are some other areas of conversation. This is what is called 'time-pass' and that is exactly what the sisters were doing sitting around a weak electric fire in Cliff Hall on a fine winter day. They had returned after attending Miss Lewis's funeral. She had been interred in the deodar- and cypress-lined cemetery for Christians on the north face of Mansuri. Their old teacher and confidante had died of complications arising from old age but it had been a peaceful passing-away.

They were speculating on the identity of the mysterious-looking woman who had been one of the mourners. Dressed in black, she had stood aside till the last moment and had then come closer to the grave to throw in a bouquet of flowers. She had a whispered conversation with the Mother Superior of the Convent and then left. When Kamlesh asked the nun about the woman she was told that she was a relative. And that was that. But it was enough to pique the curiosity of Kamlesh and Pappi.

'Could she have been the daughter Miss Lewis had once told us about?' Pappi began.

'She could have. Looked about the right age,' ventured Kamlesh.

Miss Lewis had in a moment of weakness (one of her student's babies had died of typhoid) told the sisters about her baby, who had been handed over to an orphanage in Calcutta. It was possible that Mother Superior knew more and had been given an address by Miss Lewis, which would explain the presence of her daughter at the funeral.

'Let's go and make our condolences,' Pappi said with her usual impetuousness.

'We can't. We don't know her and we don't even know if she is the daughter,' Kamlesh said.

'Someone at the funeral told me that she is staying at the Bakeman's Hotel. We could go there and try to see her. Won't do anyone any harm,' Pappi said.

As always, Kamlesh agreed, and after tea that evening they walked across to the hotel. They knew the receptionist and were told the room number and name of the woman. Her name and address as entered in the hotel register was Mrs Norma Thomas, 23 Wellesley Street, Calcutta.

Pappi knocked timidly on Mrs Thomas's door. After a while the door opened and for a moment the sisters were startled by the striking resemblance the woman bore to Miss Lewis. They explained who they were and why they had come. Mrs Thomas asked them to come into the room where she asked them to join her for a cup of tea.

They sipped their tea and in between sips Mrs Thomas told them about her life. She had grown up in an orphanage called St Andrews, and after finishing school had joined a mercantile firm as a secretary. She had married, had children and was now a widow living all by herself. Her children had migrated to Australia and came to see her once every two years. She said that they wanted her to migrate too but she wasn't going to leave Calcutta for all the tea in China, as she put it.

'Why didn't you come to see Miss Lewis in all these years?' Pappi asked.

'Well, I didn't know about her till a few years back. I then wrote a couple of times but my letters came back undelivered. I assumed she was dead till I got this telegramme the day before from Mother Superior apprising me of her death. I took the first flight to New Delhi and a taxi up here to see her for one first and last time,' Mrs Thomas told them.

'What did it feel like?' Pappi asked.

'Nothing. After all she was a total stranger, as far as I was concerned. I suppose I was simply curious.

I wanted to see what my biological mother looked like. You know, people look much better when they are dead because you can't see their eyes. It's the eyes that give people away.'

She was so matter-of-fact about the whole thing that Pappi wondered if the woman had any feelings at all. But she must have—she'd been married and had had children.

They finished their tea and Kamlesh suggested that it was time they took her leave. Mrs Thomas thanked them for coming, and that was that.

The sisters continued with their walk and eventually landed up at their shop. There they made another pot of tea, their way, and sat down to wait for the odd customer. And also for the regular gossip about town from the man nextdoor who sold toys and other gewgaws for children.

⁕

THIRTY-THREE

Life moves on a predestined course, as is believed by most, and a time comes when you can't find any means or desire to change it even while your mind can't stay still and is shouting, 'Do something, anything.' Everybody harbours pet grudges, starry-eyed dreams, often slights, imaginary or real, and waits for the day when he or she can have their revenge.

From records available, the same would seem to be the case with Babuji a.k.a. P.P. Sharma as he lounged around in the Doon Jail waiting to serve out his term. The records as usual are in the form of a loosely-kept diary and it always amazes chroniclers like me to read what people write down of their deepest, blackest thoughts and actions when they think that nobody will ever get to read them. Why they keep a diary is another mystery but it certainly comes in handy for the person trying to make sense of the life and times of anyone.

I am quoting from it because it makes my task easier, though as I have said earlier, the man wrote in a mixture of Hindi and English and wasn't a great stylist. You can't compare it to the diaries of Samuel Pepys or accounts of men like Sterne. I have, therefore, taken liberties with the language to make it more coherent and readable. But I have not taken away the dark mind that emerges from those random jottings.

Excerpts from Babuji a.k.a. P.P. Sharma's diary:

This morning the warden met me in the library to tell me that my ten years of incarceration were about to come to an end and I could apply for a release on parole with promises to be a law-abiding citizen. He said that I had been a model prisoner and that he'd be happy to say so in his report, which would give weight to my application for an early release. I had deliberately ingratiated myself to the warden by behaving in a submissive way and following all the rules. I had also put the word out through the jailor's trustees that a suitable reward awaited the warden in return for a good word. In my heart of hearts I couldn't have cared less for the man, but I realised it was important to put on appearances because it was from those that the world judged us all.

One of my perks was my evenings out in town. While my sexual urges were more or less on the wane I would, when the mood got me, visit the local brothel and 'refresh' myself . You know what I mean. And because of my free evenings I was able to see the release of my film. Later, from the papers that we got in the library, and the film magazines, I knew that the film had done well at the box-office. My assistant in Bombay sent me the weekly receipts and I knew that the money was being safely banked. Following this success I wrote and asked the director to make another one based on a story I wrote. It was again a formula film and this too did well.

Nobody but the director and my assistant knew I was in jail, and whenever the film press asked to meet me they were fobbed with one excuse or the other. I was a bit of a mystery and I enjoyed being one.

But most times, I brooded. It was that damn Pappi and her sister who were responsible for sending me to jail. If I hadn't engineered that marriage I wouldn't have been in the predicament I was in. There was no way anyone else could have got me where I was. It was a question of time, I knew, and I would get even with the two of them. I thought of plan after plan, discarding them at will, sometimes re-running them in my mind and sometimes creating outlandish plots. While it helped to pass the sleepless nights it also gave me some satisfaction that I still had the capacity to scheme. And that is what I did all those ten years behind bars.

⸺◦/◦/◦⸺

THIRTY-FOUR

Mrs Norma Thomas of 23 Wellesley Street, Second Floor, Calcutta, worked in the firm that once belonged to Moni Baba. I was told this by a person who had known her. After Moni Baba's sudden disappearance following the murder of his wife and her paramour, the firm was taken over by a distant relative who had been an employee. He managed to bring some order into things and the firm prospered.

She had joined some time after Moni Baba's disappearance and so knew nothing much about him except for the fact that he was the boss who had upped and disappeared. Office gossip had it that he could be declared dead only after seven years and as far as legal matters went he was officially still around somewhere.

Like most young Anglo-Indian girls she was an efficient secretary and was able to work her way up the pool to become secretary to the managing director, Sudanshu Banerjee. After seven years, legal proceedings were initiated, and Somdeb Banerjee was finally declared dead and the firm in effect became Sudanshu Banerjee's proprietary concern as there were no other claimants to the business or the property.

Under his stewardship the firm prospered. He changed the old name, brought in new technology and managers fresh from business schools. He also shifted his headquarters from Calcutta to New Delhi, which was fast becoming the economic hub of the country.

However, Mrs Thomas chose to remain behind and manage the Calcutta office that had by then been reduced to a mere guesthouse for visiting executives. It was a comfortable job in that there wasn't much to do except arrange for air and rail tickets and cars to ferry the executives from place to place.

By that time, Mrs Thomas's children wanted to migrate to Australia to where all their friends were making a beeline. Her husband had died and she had little say in what the young people wanted to do. With her savings she bought them tickets for Sydney and off they went to seek their fortune.

She lived alone in the flat on Wellesley, cooked her own meals, had a cleaning woman come in every day to do the dishes and the dusting and swabbing. On weekends she went to the movies with her old friend Mrs D'Cruz, another widow. She was a member of the American Library on S.N. Banerjee Road and would borrow books and read the latest American publications. For a simple office secretary she was quite well informed about world affairs but there was no one she could talk to or discuss with, the momentous events taking place all over the world.

Just around that time cable TV was introduced to Calcutta. After a lot of persuasion by Mrs D'Cruz, Mrs Thomas decided to invest in a colour TV and subscribe to cable. The idiot box changed her life. Initially, she was a regular watcher of CNN and BBC. But soon she began to surf channels and would rush home from office to catch the latest on the soaps. She also discovered Hindi soaps and, like the millions of viewers, she was so fascinated by the small screen that she hardly ever stirred outside except to go to work. She stopped her Saturday evening outings and, much to her friend's disappointment, also stopped attending Sunday church.

She particularly liked a programme that dealt with

unsolved murders and assorted mysteries that had confounded people for a long time. It gave her mind a chance to gallop along the realms of the possible and the seemingly impossible.

On one of those days she saw a story about the mysterious murder of an old woman who lived all alone in an apartment in New York. The story was told through her Persian cat, who could recognise the murderer, but the police were completely at a loss and were unable to find clues and evidence that would lead them to the murderer. Eventually, they take on the services of a clairvoyant woman. She tells them what she thinks the killer looks like after talking to the cat and seeing the man in the cat's eyes and over time the police nab the man who confesses to the murder.

Slowly, Mrs Thomas grew convinced she was clairvoyant and had certain psychic powers. So strong was her conviction that she began to practise first on her friend Mrs D'Cruz. She would ring her up and tell her the colour of the dress she was wearing or what she had eaten for lunch and such other minor matters. Mrs D'Cruz was suitably impressed. So much so that she began to spread the word in the small world she inhabited about Mrs Thomas's 'mysterious powers'.

Soon people began to call on old Mrs Thomas to ask her to find things they'd lost, to identify thieves, and such. Most times Mrs Thomas would accurately describe the house of the inquirer and tell her or him where the missing object was lying.

The difficult part was when some women came to ask her to describe the woman who their husband was sleeping with.

Mrs Lewis would hem and haw and give vague answers that would partly satisfy her 'customers'. Yes, she had 'clients' now, because to control the rush of people who came to her asking about their missing cats and dogs, errant servants and such trivial matters, she had began to charge a small fee. Some of the more satisfied people would give her larger amounts when and if she solved their problems.

That was all very good because now she could afford to keep a fulltime servant who also helped out with the daily bazaar and kept her company as she watched TV virtually day and night.

Her 'fame' spread in the locality. When she went out to catch the tram that took her to work, the neighbourhood boys would run for cover. To them she was some kind of a witch and any eye contact with her meant very bad luck. She scared them out of their wits though there were some bold ones who, for a dare or a wager, would run behind her and pinch her to see if she was real. Mrs Thomas, essentially a kind-hearted woman, would often chase the boys away with a swipe of her umbrella and stare into their eyes to frighten them further.

Soon, lines of people formed outside her house

from early in the morning on Sundays and holidays. She did not give consultations, as she proudly said, on her office days. One of her more 'satisfied' clients eventually reported her 'super powers' to the tantric, Shankar, in Bhawanipore.

Shankar took the news with a pinch of salt but nevertheless agreed to go and meet her. That meeting became the turning point of this narrative.

⚬⚬⚬

THIRTY-FIVE

It was a sunny morning when P.P. Sharma walked out of the Doon Jail. Life in jail had made him lose the surplus fat on his waist, and the brand new sharkskin suit fitted him to a tee. His shiny, tasselled shoes clicked on the asphalt for the few feet he walked before getting into a spanking new Honda City. A man opened the door for him and he slipped into the back.

The warden and his flunkeys stood respectfully to one side, and with a desultory wave to them, P.P. Sharma was driven off by a smartly dressed chauffeur. The man who had opened the door for him was his secretary and confidant and had managed his business affairs while he cooled his heels in jail.

No one else saw him disappear into the distance that morning and soon the car was snaking its way through the Mohand Pass and onto the Delhi Road. For breakfast they stopped at a point midway where Sharma was delighted to see a modern looking restaurant with well-laid out lawns and gardens, a neat and clean toilet and reasonable food to go with it. He had remarked to his secretary about the width and smoothness of the road and was told that the government was building a six-lane highway that would reduce the driving time between Delhi and Dehradun to about three hours, instead of the six at present. 'So things are looking up, finally,' Sharma had remarked wryly.

In Delhi, Sharma checked into a posh hotel where a Russian woman was waiting for him. It had been a long time since he had had sex and while the spirit was willing the flesh had weakened. He took off his clothes, had a shower and asked the woman to pour him a drink from the bottle of Scotch kept for that purpose. He looked at her appreciatively and couldn't help but marvel at her trim but full figure.

'Do you have a friend?' he asked the woman.

'Da,' she said.

'Send for her,' he ordered his secretary.

The other woman was ushered in shortly. She too was a statuesque blonde and as tall and busty as the first one. Sharma signalled them to take their clothes off, and the women began to strip to piped music.

Soon they were kissing and fondling each other and as Sharma grew aroused he beckoned his secretary to come and fondle his penis.

The women came and lay down next to him and made love to each other. He fondled the breasts of one of them, while his secretary commenced to give him a blowjob. It had been too long for Sharma and he came fast and was soon snoring. The women were paid off and escorted out of the room by the secretary. Sharma had finally arrived in the big city.

❦

THIRTY-SIX

In Calcutta, Shankar the tantric went to meet Mrs Thomas. He was so obviously a holy man that Mrs Thomas was momentarily confused. Why would he want to see her, of all people? They started with preliminary greetings in Bengali—hers with a Bengali accent—and then Shankar surprised her by telling her all about her mother, Mrs Lewis. The man told her about Mrs Lewis's elopement, the death of her father as a young man and Mrs Lewis's life in the Mansuri convent school. And then he said, 'Now you tell me about my life.'

Mrs Thomas went into a trance as she closed her eyes. Like in a film she saw Shankar growing up in

Calcutta slums, leading the rough and ready life of a petty thief and a street thug. She told him all about that and then about his travels in the mountains with two other people whom she didn't know, his life with another tantric high up, somewhere in snowclad mountains.

The story just kept rolling off her tongue and Shankar was impressed enough to ask her to stop. She then opened her eyes and blinked a couple of times like someone who has woken up from a deep sleep.

'I think you are a true *siddhi*,' he told her.

'What is a siddhi?' she asked him.

'Someone who has powers that other humans don't,' he translated. 'Use them carefully, and only for the good of others.' Then he smiled at her and left.

For some time after that Mrs Thomas sat in silence wondering what made her different from other people. When and how had she got these powers? What had begun as a minor experiment had now become some kind of a superpower to be used at will by her. Her meeting with Shankar had further convinced her that she must use her newfound powers with caution. If she didn't do that she would lose her mind, he had said.

When Mrs D'Cruz came to call on her she told her about her meeting with Shankar. Her friend agreed with what Shankar had said. She told Mrs Thomas that she had heard of people who misused these powers and made life hell for themselves. The two women decided to keep Mrs Thomas's secret, a secret.

Shankar met Moni Baba later that day and told him about his extraordinary meeting with Mrs Thomas. Both men agreed that such kind of people did exist and while they may not have gone through the rigorous discipline of a true tantric, they nevertheless acquired the same powers.

Moni Baba wrote about Shankar's meeting in his diary and more or less forgot about it. He decided to push on to Allahabad. There, the city was beginning to hot up and the loo, the hot, dusty wind that blew all day long, was picking up in strength. It was well nigh impossible to stir out of the house after ten in the morning unless one had an air-conditioned car. But there was nowhere in particular that Moni Baba wanted to go. He was quite happy to stay indoors where a desert cooler provided him with some comfort from the burning heat outside.

⋘◦◦◦⋙

THIRTY-SEVEN

More and more people in Allahabad were becoming victims of local thugs who the media called the land mafia. In the Civil Lines area, where people once owned palatial houses with big lawns and gardens, a change was fast becoming apparent.

Most of these properties wore the desolate and uncared look of houses owned by absentee or deceased landlords.

In addition, there were often disputes among those who had inherited them. This is where the so-called land mafia came in. It was a phenomenon which was becoming quite widespread all over urban India. In Bombay, Madras, Calcutta and bigger towns, real estate dealers hired goons to either frighten the old people off or buy them off at ridiculously low prices. If there was any resistance, murder was often the solution.

Allahabad, home to an assorted bunch of idlers and people who made a dubious living off visiting pilgrims, developed a reputation for also being one of the best places to recruit 'shooters', knifers, extortionists and generally men who would do dark deeds for a fee. The newspapers were full of stories about small-town crooks who had made it to the exalted status of 'dons' of the underworld.

Moni Baba knew all about this because he too had been approached by builders to sell off his bungalow. Since he lived alone with only a man servant, the bungalow, built in the old colonial fashion, was really too big for them. Because Moni Baba did not pay much attention to maintenance and repairs it was badly damaged in parts. He was quite tempted to sell it and move on but the builder he met got his dander up when he threatened Moni Baba.

Moni Baba was not a man who could be easily intimidated. He told the builder where to go in no uncertain terms.

One hot morning, Moni Baba had finished his morning ablutions, prayers and yoga exercises and was sitting down to a breakfast of yogurt and parathas in the verandah of the bungalow. He saw two men on a motorcycle roar into his compound. The pillion rider whipped out a revolver and took two shots at Moni Baba before the driver wheeled the motorcycle around and left in a trail of dust. Fortunately, both the shots missed Moni Baba though one of them knocked his food to the ground.

That was enough to make the man lose his temper. His servant, who had heard the shots, came running out of the kitchen which was a bit away from the house. He was relieved when he saw that Moni Baba was all right though the remains of his breakfast lay scattered all over the verandah floor.

In a cold voice, Moni Baba asked him to take the car out of the garage. The servant, who also doubled as a driver, did that and the two men set off in hot pursuit of the men on the motorcycle.

Moni Baba had recognised the two thugs. He knew they were from the Muthiganj area, not too far from Alopi Bagh where Bhagwan had once owned a house. In those days Moni Baba was often visited by local hoods. These dadas sought his blessings before embarking on one criminal enterprise after the other.

The way Moni Baba saw things, there was no difference between criminals and others. They were all God's creatures or so he told himself. He knew quite a few of these thugs. He had even visited their homes, and he guided his driver to take him to one such house.

The man he went to see was called Bhola Pehelwan who was once a wrestler. Bhola Pehelwan had made a name for himself all over in the area for of his wrestling skills. But time, age, drink and loose living took their toll. He then began to do what former wrestlers did. He opened an akhara, a gymnasium where young wrestlers trained in the finer aspects of their sport.

In his role as a guru, he soon had an impressive following of young toughs. To keep them in line he offered to give protection to the city's merchants for a fee. That was his source of revenue, which kept him and his cohorts in booze and food and the odd prostitute.

Bhola received Moni Baba in the *angan*, the courtyard of his house where he was lounging on a charpoy laid out under a sprawling neem tree. A table fan pushed some air around but even at that time of the morning it was hot and sultry, and the fan's efforts did nothing for the obese, pot-bellied Bhola. He was sweating profusely and one of his students waved a fan over him while another pressed his feet and massaged his legs. A glass, half full of rum with ice in it, was clutched in his hands and a cigarette dangled from his lips.

Of course, he didn't recognise the clean-shaven and tonsured Moni Baba. What he saw was a middle-aged man who was apparently well-to-do. He noted the man's gold wristwatch, smart bush shirt and trousers, and highly polished sandals. After running his eyes from head to toe and back again to make eye contact with Moni Baba, he raised his eyebrows in a questioning mode.

Many years ago Bhola had knifed a man and then taken shelter in the ashram with the blessings of Moni Baba. He had confessed in great detail to the murder and also to others organised by him. Moni Baba had explained to him through hand signals and short notes that it was nothing in the bigger scheme of things. That was his karma and he had to do all the nasty things he had described. God was his guide and so he should feel no remorse or guilt.

From that time onward Bhola had become a devotee and would often donate large sums to the ashram. The word had gone out that the ashram was under the protection of Bhola.

Moni Baba, in his new avatar, told Bhola that he had been sent by Moni Baba. Bhola managed to sit upright as a sign of respect for the holy man. He asked about Moni Baba's health and when told that he was doing well, looked relieved. Moni Baba told him what had happened that morning and he described the perpetrators. Bhola immediately recognised the duo who worked for another gang. He assured him that the matter would be taken care of and there was nothing to fear.

The next morning, two men were found shot dead in front of Moni Baba's bungalow. They had obviously been shot elsewhere and their bodies dumped at the bungalow. That it was a gangland killing was made clear by the way the men had been shot. Single shots to the area just behind the ear.

The police came, asked a few desultory questions of the bystanders and left with the bodies. They knew who the two men were and also knew that they were wanted criminals. There was little or no point in chasing the matter further. And that was the last of any intimidation to Moni Baba.

THIRTY-EIGHT

P.P. Sharma's secretary had been scouting around for a house for his boss. He found an independent bungalow in New Friends Colony, a fast-growing upmarket suburb of New Delhi. Once inside its high walls, your privacy was guaranteed, P.P. Sharma noted in his diary.

It was also the kind of neighbourhood where people

were hardly interested in their neighbours. It was all part of the new culture that had invaded the once sleepy, government town. Now, the rich lived in south Delhi and points further south in large farmhouses, and kept fierce-looking dogs and armed men to guard their premises. This suited Sharma perfectly too.

His two servants, who had served time with him for the botched murder of his deaf and dumb servant, acted as the cook and gardener-cum-chowkidar. There was no interaction with anyone and there was no need for it. If one wanted to eat, one rang for it from the numerous restaurants in the area and it came right to your doorstep. If you wanted booze, women or anything else, all you had to have were the right numbers and they too were home-delivered.

It was in this house that the plans for his next evil act were laid. He was old enough to realise that there wasn't any need to acquire more wealth. What he wanted now was to quench his thirst for revenge. It was a one-point agenda and in his mind it was like a festering sore. It needed to be lanced so that the pus would run out, relieve the pressure on his brain and bring him peace.

Excerpts from his diary:

I am comfortably and, more important, safely living in this house in New Friends Colony. I don't know why it is called Friends Colony. It is the most unfriendly place on earth. But that's fine with me. I don't want to make any new friends at this time of my life.

If and when I want company, especially female, I send for them through my secretary. He has a list of phone numbers of the best prostitutes in town. I spend time watching DVDs on my big-screen TV. At all other times I keep thinking of how to take my revenge for the ten years spent in jail.

I am sending my secretary to Mansuri to see how things are going with the sisters. Since no one knows him there, he can move around freely without drawing any suspicion to himself. I have asked him to check into the best hotel there and make friends with local people. He will pass himself off as a film producer from Bombay who is looking around for locations for a new film he plans to shoot. I have instructed him to also spread the word that he might be interested in buying some suitable property.

(A later entry)

The secretary has returned after a two-week stay in Mansuri. He tells me that the sisters are looking very well. He has managed to make friends with a shopkeeper who doesn't like them but pretends to be a friend. Apparently, many years ago, when the sisters were younger he was rejected by Kamlesh after he had asked her father for her hand in marriage. He has never forgotten the insult, my secretary tells me. This is all to the good. I think I will be able to use him effectively.

The secretary also tells me that the sisters might be interested in selling their property in Mansuri. This he has learnt from his newfound friend. The reason, the man explained, is that the sisters find the cold too much to bear and wish to move out to the plains. Also, property prices in Mansuri are at an all-time high and not a day passes without someone or the other selling his old and dilapidated house for a fortune. Even the old servants' quarters, and ruins which once housed rickshaws and coolies, are being bought for large sums and then converted into hotels and posh apartments.

When I asked my secretary the reason behind this boom in prices he said that there was a legal ruling which had banned the construction of new properties. However, old properties could be dismantled and new ones built in their place.

Obviously, the sisters knew about this. Their house, Cliff Hall, is located at the Mall in a prime location and has, besides the main building, servants' quarters, big lawns that were once tennis courts and a delightful view overlooking the Doon Valley. As someone said, location, location and location are the only criteria for buying property.

—⟨o/o/o⟩—

THIRTY-NINE

It was a simple coincidence that Mrs Thomas also landed up in Mansuri to spend that summer. She had booked a set of rooms at the house of a writer who kept paying guests to supplement his meagre royalties. The writer, yours truly, had lived in Calcutta in his youth where he once worked for a newspaper. He had spread the word through friends that he kept paying guests but he wanted the quiet type who ate their meals on time, did not stay up at all hours, did not demand tandoori chicken at a moment's notice, and generally minded their own business.

The coincidence was that Moni Baba had booked another set of rooms in the same house under his real name, Somdeb Bannerjee.

It was a largish bungalow built sometime in the 1830s and was located on a spur with an awe-inspiring view of the valley. Mr Bannerjee travelled with his own cook and kept mostly to his rooms except when he went out for his evening walk.

Living under the same roof does make it impossible to avoid meeting people. One evening, as Mr Bannerjee was setting off for his evening walk, dressed rather nattily in a light-blue pullover and grey worsted trousers, he ran into Mrs Thomas who too was planning to make her evening visit to the town where she had coffee with the sisters in their small shop.

Except for the nuns, they were the only people she could call friends. The old lady had ordered a taxi from the town to take her up to Picture Palace, now a closed-down cinema hall at the eastern end of the Mall, when she encountered Mr Bannerjee. They exchanged greetings in the cold manner of people who are forced to share space in the same house, and Mr Bannerjee set off briskly for his walk. In time, the taxi came to drive Mrs Thomas to her rendezvous.

Moni Baba's walks took him past the shop owned by the two sisters and he had made it a rule to glance inside to see that everything was shipshape. He would then drop in at the Kwality restaurant, located rather strategically at a higher level than the Mall, order a coffee and admire the sunset.

It was the height of summer and the Mall was a busy place with throngs of people dressed in their best clothes and the latest fashions from the big cities in the plains, managing to stroll through the crowded street. Mr Bannerjee, sitting at his table in Kwality's, had a bird's eye view of the Mall and the sisters' shop and he enjoyed the passing show as he leisurely sipped his coffee.

He saw Mrs Thomas making her way slowly to the sisters' shop. She went inside and he knew she would be there for the better part of an hour, during which he guessed the women would gossip about people they knew in common. What he couldn't guess was the other things they talked about.

Mr Bannerjee had heard of Mrs Thomas and noted what Shankar had told him about her in his diary. He had a vague idea that the lady in question was the same woman who was sitting and chatting with the sisters.

Another man who was watching the shop was the man who owned the shop across the road. He was the one befriended by Sharma's secretary and it was his given task to keep an eye on who came and went. He would then report all that to the secretary who in turn would send the information on to his master in New Delhi. The shopkeeper, in his turn, was being watched by Mr Bannerjee.

❦❦❦

FORTY

In any murder, events and people involved are more often than not illogically placed in recall. There is no pattern, contrary to what mystery and murder writers would have us believe. The police know that, and that is why so many murders remain unsolved. Despite the advances in forensics, DNA testing and so on, the fact remains that it takes a long time for anyone to eventually deduce and conclude a murder case. Or, the murderer, in a gesture of bitter remorse, confesses.

Or, perhaps, in some instances there are those who have psychic and paranormal powers who can help.

A lanky police officer called Ishwari Dutt was, in Mansuri's circles, simply known as I.D. He was posted to the town in what was to be the last phase of his service. He had planned to retire to a small farm where he would spend his old age growing vegetables.

At the time of his posting he had no idea that the last years of his otherwise humdrum career would end in a blaze of glory. Or, as he thought and often told people, 'a big headache'.

What made I.D. the least likely crime detective was the fact that he had no training or experience in dealing with complicated murder cases. In his career he had been witness to shootouts between two rival gangs and in his role as a witness he was quite happy to see the criminals eliminating each other. Once, he had been in an encounter in which he witnessed the shooting of an unarmed man by his fellow policemen. The dead man was later taken and dumped near a railway station and the police claimed that they had to shoot him as he was trying to evade arrest in several cases of murder, extortion and rape.

That was the way the police worked.

But here the story is getting a bit ahead of the events. The town boasted of one or two real estate dealers who could be called professionals. However, there were quite a few people ranging from paanwallahs to hotel guides who styled themselves as dealers but who didn't know the A or B or Cs of the business. They would take the prospective buyer to a prospective seller who, in turn, would consult the big operators and these small men would be fobbed of with a paltry commission for their effort.

Among such operators was a man called Khosla who would pass himself off as a representative of some newspaper or a contractor or a public relations expert. It all depended on what he needed to be at the moment. He had good relations with the police because he regularly sneaked to them about the various nefarious and not-so-nefarious activities going on in the town. He also had good relations with the clerks and officials in the kutchery because he arranged for suitable commissions for them. He was what could be described as a small-time fixer— and they can be found in most towns in droves. They are an oily and ingratiating lot who worm their way into people's confidence, and at this, Khosla excelled.

He was a great one for touching people's feet in a show of reverence, and that did go down well with the older people who thought Khosla was a well-brought up young man. This is an important operating tool of conmen. They earn the trust of older people because older people, in the main, are lonely, insecure and often lack the knowledge or the brains to manage their business affairs. It is an aspect of growing old as much as disease and senility is part and parcel of aging.

In small towns like Mansuri there are many old men and women who are waiting for such operators to come and make suckers of them. And the reason is simple—they don't trust their nearest and dearest, or, there is no one they can call nearest or dearest. And nearly all of them have assets that are worth a fortune.

❦

FORTY-ONE

Khosla had a most effective routine. He would begin his day early to catch most of the elderly on their morning walks or while they were visiting temples or gurdwaras or mosques. He stayed away from the Christian community because he didn't speak English and that was a handicap in his line of work. Old ladies would gladly take up his offer of a helping hand as they climbed treacherous stairs leading to their choice of places of worship, on their stiff, arthritic limbs. Old men would often rest a hand on his shoulder as he guided them along a tricky slope.

Everyone who knew Khosla said he was an affable, charming and considerate young man. Of course, it helped that he did not smoke or drink or eat paan. And if any one asked him he would proudly claim to be a strict vegetarian who fasted every Tuesday and touched his forehead on a temple doorstep every day depending on which part of the town he was. Needless to say, but it has to be said: the man was a hypocrite.

Khosla was a regular to the sisters' shop. He would drop in every evening to make his usual inquiries about their health, and ask them if he could do anything for them. Often, they would entrust some small chore like the payment of telephone, electricity and water bills, which he would carry out with alacrity. Like others, the sisters too thought he was a really nice man.

Often, they would tell him where they had been on a Sunday. And this is how Khosla learnt that they were visiting a tantric in Rishikesh.

Mr Bannerjee knew about these visits and he also knew who the tantric was. It was his friend Shankar. From him he was to learn that the sisters were thinking of selling their property and buying a place somewhere on the banks of the Ganga where they could spend their old age in meditation and prayer.

Shankar told them that it was not a good idea. The

sale was fraught with danger and the sisters were warned to be very careful in their dealings. But they had told him that they were sick and fed up with the way they lived and the people around them.

It is easy enough to tell someone something for his or her good but rare for that person to follow your advice. The sisters were no different from a whole lot of people. They listened to everyone in their polite way but did exactly what they wanted. And in doing that they would be so secretive that even the many gods they worshipped would hang their heads in shame at their naivety. Such was their nature and who is to say why.

Later that evening, as Mr Bannerjee sat down to his spare supper, he heard the television set go on in what was called the drawing room. It was the only place in the house where visitors could meet or watch TV or listen to music. But since most people were the retiring type, who preferred the company of a book or a magazine in their rooms, the TV was seldom put on. So he was a bit curious about the noise of the machine and after supper decided to walk across and see who was the guest who preferred the company of what he secretly called the idiot box.

It was Mrs Thomas. And to make matters more intriguing was the fact that she had switched on a Bengali channel. She was watching the news and it was all about Calcutta with a bit of national interest thrown in. She had smiled at Mr Bannerjee when he walked into the room and that could be construed as a greeting of sorts.

He went and sat on the rocking chair facing the TV. After the news programme, a santoor recital by Pandit Shiv Kumar Sharma, the maestro, came on and the two of them sat back to enjoy the performance.

I walked in just as the performance came to an end. I waved a hello to both of them and said, 'I see you've met.'

'Well, not formally,' Mr Bannerjee said.

'I see. Well, this is Mrs Thomas, and ma'am, this is Mr Bannerjee,' I said.

'From Calcutta?' Mrs Thomas asked in Bengali.

Rather taken aback at her use of Bengali, Mr Bannerjee nodded and smiled.

Then she surprised him further when she said that he also had a house in Allahabad. Mrs Thomas was showing off her psychic powers. But before the conversation could proceed further the lights went out, a regular feature in Mansuri.

Outside, there was the sound of thunder and as I went to get a box of matches from the kitchen I saw flashes in the southern sky. Another pre-monsoon storm was brewing and invariably, the electricity people would throw the main switches to save their systems from damage. I scrambled around in the dark, found a box of matches and came back to the drawing room to light the kerosene lamp kept there for that purpose. The storm was soon upon us and as the rain began its hammering on the corrugated galvanised iron roof of the house, all conversation dried up.

The three of us huddled around the lamp and looked out of the windows to see the play of lightning in the sky. It was a quite a sight and though I must have seen these storms hundreds of times I am always enthralled by the way the lightning snakes across the sky or comes shooting down to strike some place in the valley. Once, the house was hit by a bolt, and every single window pane was blown to bits. And another time the tall pine on the western approach to the house was torn asunder.

Mrs Thomas broke into my thoughts, asking, 'Has the house a lightning conductor?'

'Unfortunately, no,' I told her.

'Well then, we should have some protection, shouldn't we?' she said.

'I suppose so, but they say that lightning doesn't strike the same place twice,' Bannerjee said. It looked like he was reading my mind.

'I don't believe that because I know the spire of the St James Church in Calcutta has been hit a number of times,' Mrs Thomas put in.

'But that would happen. The spire acts as a lightning conductor,' Mr Bannerjee said. 'Besides, it is the tallest structure for miles around.'

I remembered the church as it stood in one corner

of the Maidan, the vast expanse of green that people like to describe as the lungs of Calcutta. It was also the place where children gathered to play cricket, and lovers stole kisses as they sat under the sprawling shade of all kinds of trees. And at night the 'bush guerrillas' or streetwalkers did their business in the darkness. Behind the bushes, you know.

'There are ghosts in this house,' Mrs Thomas said, apropos of nothing.

'What?' said Mr Bannerjee.

'Ghosts. You know the spirits of people who are either killed in tragic circumstances or condemned to purgatory.'

I chipped in my two bits and pointed out that I had never seen any in all my years of living in the house. And neither had my parents, I added for effect.

'Rubbish,' said Mr Bannerjee. 'I mean, ghosts. They are all figments of people's imaginations.'

But the exchange between Mrs Thomas and Mr Bannerjee was just another example of how people agree to disagree. The storm blew away, and after some time, the lights came back. There wasn't much to talk about and we all went to our rooms after perfunctory good nights.

FORTY-TWO

Khosla did what he always did. When he heard that the sisters were thinking of selling their house he went to the biggest broker in town. He told him that he could convince the sisters and a sale was possible. They only had to find a buyer. The broker had dealt with people like Khosla and he knew the man could be bought for a few thousand for doing the legwork. He also knew that it would be impossible for him to approach the sisters. This was because he had tried it once and they had told him in no uncertain terms to never ever raise the subject again.

The big broker knew about the inquiries being made by Babuji's secretary. The man who had a shop opposite the sisters had told him someone was interested in the property. The shopkeeper was summoned. He came as fast as he could. He sensed a big fat commission: greed was the only motivating factor in his life.

Following the shopkeeper's call, Babuji's secretary came up from Delhi. On arrival, he wasted no time and asked the broker what the going price was. The broker told him it could be anywhere between four to four-and-a-half crore. Then Khosla was summoned and he said he could take the secretary to meet the sisters. The time was set for 5 pm.

Everyone knew the sisters did not meet anyone inside their house. But Khosla was adamant that he would arrange the meeting.

In town, it was well known that the sisters left their house by 6 pm, to open the shop around half an hour later. So, Khosla assumed, he would have an hour to discuss the deal.

When they reached Cliff Hall, Khosla and the secretary found themselves standing outside the grilled door with the elder sister, Kamlesh, asking Khosla what was it that he wanted.

Khosla made his obeisance and in his oily manner asked if he could come in because the matter he had to discuss could not be discussed through the closed grille of the door. Kamlesh hesitated and asked to know what there was to discuss which could not be done through the closed grille. Khosla insisted in his most persuasive way and, just when Kamlesh was about to tell him to go away, Pappi came up and asked her what the matter was.

Kamlesh explained in a whisper that Khosla wanted to talk to them but he had come with a stranger and they wanted to come inside the house. Pappi thought that there was nothing wrong with that and, after all, it was broad daylight despite the fact that Mansuri was enveloped in a thick mist. Reluctantly, Kamlesh opened the grille door.

The two men came in and respectfully touched the

feet of the sisters. They were then asked to sit down on a sofa that had seen much wear and tear. The rusty springs sqeaked as the two men sank into them. The sisters sat on two stools and looked inquiringly at Khosla.

Khosla began by telling them that he had heard that they were interested in selling Cliff Hall and the land appurtenant to it.

'Now where did you hear that?' Kamlesh asked in her mild manner.

'That's what the gossip in the bazaar is, Behenji,' Khosla explained.

'We will pay you a good price,' the man accompanying him said.

'And what would be a good price?' Pappi asked.

'Whatever you say. I mean, within reason,' the man replied.

There was complete silence after that. After a while, Kamlesh walked to the door, opened it and gestured to the two men to leave. They got up and silently left.

Outside the house and once they were on the road, the man berated Khosla for bringing him all the way up from Delhi for nothing. Khosla told him he was certain that the sisters wanted to sell. He pleaded for more time and said he was confident that he would be able to convince them. The man laughed at him and went off to his hotel. *(All this is from Khosla's account to the police after the murder.)*

FORTY-THREE

That evening the sisters went to their shop as usual. Soon, they were joined by Mrs Thomas for coffee. Mr Bannerjee sat at his favourite table at Kwality's sipping his cappuccino and looking down at the crowd on the Mall.

The mist had become thicker and visibility was restricted to a few yards. Kamlesh said that it was going to rain soon and Pappi nodded in agreement. Mrs Thomas then said she'd better be getting along as it wouldn't do to get caught in the rain. After their goodbyes and hugs, Mrs Thomas walked out of the shop and began the short walk to the taxi stand. From there she took a taxi and drove to the writer's house.

Mr Bannerjee too sensed the change in weather and took the short cut down and was soon in his rooms.

The rain broke in all its fury and the lights went off. Each of them ate their dinner by candlelight. Mrs Thomas in the dining room, and Mr Bannerjee in his room. Mrs Thomas asked the serving man where the master was and he replied saying he was in his room entertaining some friends from town. She wondered aloud when the lights would, if ever, come back so she could watch the news before turning in. The man said he didn't know but he was hopeful the rain would stop soon.

It turned out he was quite right and just when Mrs Thomas finished her after-dinner coffee, the rain stopped hammering on the roof and the lights came back. She moved to the drawing room, put on the TV and began to listen to the news on the Bengali channel.

In his room, Mr Bannerjee heard the TV come on and thought it would be a good idea to while away some time with Mrs Thomas. He then proceeded to join her there and sat down on the rocking chair.

In my room, my friends and I were well into our cups. They couldn't possibly leave the house in the driving rain, so the drinking session had been gladly prolonged. Besides, somebody remembered that it was my birthday the next day and an impromptu party of sorts was soon in progress.

Among the three men present was the police inspector called I.D. He was well into his bottle of whisky which had been donated for the evening by the town's bootlegger. He was regaling us with stories about his experiences as a policeman. He lamented the fact that he couldn't make a cent in Mansuri because there was no crime and hence no criminals.

In the plains, he told us, he could rake in as much as three to four lakh a month. And, he added for effect, this was when he was only moderately dishonest. A policeman had to be corrupt if he was to get along in his career, he explained. The big boys could take home double the amount, he said.

I wanted to know how he hid his ill-gotten loot from his superiors and learnt that his superiors were on the take too. It is a jolly big family, the police force, I.D. told us, and gulped down another drink. That should give you an idea of the kind of man I.D. was. He was the type who pushed doors with 'pull' written on them.

In the drawing room, Mr Bannerjee waited patiently for the news to finish before opening conversation.

He said, 'Rather stormy tonight, isn't it?'

'Yes,' Mrs Thomas replied. 'It's quite nice like this. Better than the heat of the plains.'

'Oh, yes. Anytime.'

'So, how did your day go?' Mrs Thomas asked.

'Quietly. And yours?'

'Quietly.'

Then they lapsed into silence and looked at the TV screen without quite registering what was on. Like most people who sit in front of a TV, they didn't feel the need for conversation. A chance visitor looking at them would have thought them to be a happily-or-otherwise married couple who at the end of their lives had little or nothing to say to each other. An idiot box that makes civilised conversation redundant.

But it also has its redeeming features. It can entertain, inform and in the case of Mrs Thomas, wake up the various unknown powers that reside in the mind. As she often told her close friends, it was the telly that had taught them to her.

⸺◦◦◦⸻

FORTY-FOUR

Outside, the radio-set in the police jeep crackled to life. The driver picked up the mouthpiece and acknowledged that he was receiving. The police controller on the other end told him to get the sahab on the line. The driver walked towards the house where I.D. was sitting and drinking with his friends. He told him about the radio, and I.D., groggy with drink, said, 'Fuck it. Answer it yourself.'

'I.D., it must be important,' I intervened. 'Go and answer it.'

I.D. mumbled some profanity, managed to struggle to his feet and, leaning heavily on the driver, walked off towards the jeep. He was helped in and the moment he sat down he promptly fell asleep. The driver told the controller that they were on their way back to the thana.

Because of this incident no one in the house, especially I, Mrs Thomas and Mr Bannerjee, knew about the events that unfolded that night. Also, because I.D. didn't sober up till well after midnight, the bodies of the dead sisters weren't actually discovered till later the next day.

From what the world learnt and the press reported, the police were informed by the chowkidar of the nearest neighbour that it was strange that the door of the sisters' house was unlocked and there were no lights on. He also told them that he had gone and knocked on the door but there had been no response from inside.

The chowkidar was an honest and simple man who had been working for more than fifty years for the sisters' neighbour. He also ran errands for the two women from time to time and in general kept an eye on the house. The police, as is their wont, said they would have a look into the matter. The chowkidar returned and told Rajni, the neighbour, who told her husband, Mantri, the photographer.

They also thought it strange that the sisters had left the main door open because they never went out of the house without locking it with a strong padlock. They had been doing this for such a long time that anyone who knew them would immediately find something amiss if they didn't.

Mantri and his wife pondered over the matter and because it was raining cats and dogs thought it best to let the matter rest till the morning. They went to sleep, naively secure in the belief that the matter had been reported to the police and the police would be doing the needful. They were law-abiding citizens who had faith in the khaki brigade. As events unfolded, they realised how wrong they had been all their lives.

The police, as it turned out, were doing nothing. The officer on night duty had heard the chowkidar out and sent him off. He had also had a few tots and because it was raining didn't see any point in walking all the way to the sisters' house. He didn't want to risk catching a cold. The officer who took over from him in the morning would do the follow-up, if needed.

Because of this curious turn of events, a whole day went by without any further inquiry being made. It was only when the sisters did not turn up the following evening to open their shop that their neighbour, a fellow shopkeeper, thought of making some investigations. He rang up Mantri and was told he was out of town and wouldn't be back till later in the night. The shopkeeper, a diminutive and shy man who always stayed away from any kind of trouble, decided to wait for Mantri to get back before going to the police.

The chowkidar, however, was a more determined man. He went to the police station once again and complained about the lack of action. This time he complained directly to I.D. who, now sobered up, sensed immediately that there was some substance in the old man's concern. After asking him a few questions he instructed a sub-inspector and two constables to go to Cliff Hall and have a look around and report back.

The three men went to the sisters' house. They walked through the open door, walked around the empty rooms, inspected the bathroom and, after a cursory search, went back and reported to I.D. that there was no one inside the house. By that time Mantri had come back from his outstation trip and, goaded by his wife and the shopkeeper, decided to take some initiative in the matter.

I.D. was again approached and he told them that his men had found nothing. Mantri persisted and when the chowkidar, who had accompanied the police team, complained that no one had looked into the kitchen which was bolted from the outside, I.D. got up, walked to his jeep and drove up to Cliff Hall himself, accompanied by some policemen. By this time, it was almost ten o'clock in the night.

It had been raining the whole day and Mrs Thomas and Mr Bannerjee had decided to avoid their evening outings. They spent the time sitting around the TV set, ate their dinner and were sound asleep just around the time I.D. and his police team entered Cliff Hall. I had some people over, and the birthday celebrations from the evening before resumed with gusto on that fateful night.

—◦◦◦—

FORTY-FIVE

According to the police report, the team entered the house and went towards the locked kitchen door. They drew the bolts and opened the door. Inside, they saw the two sisters lying dead on the floor. The preliminary examination showed that they had been strangulated by one or more persons. This was clear from the bruises around their throats.

They were in their nightclothes and had been dragged from some other room—possibly the drawing room—because their clothes and feet were covered in dust. The house itself was in a mess and had not been dusted or cleaned for days, if not weeks. Cobwebs had formed all over the woodwork, the windowpanes were grimy with dirt, the paintwork on the doors and window frames was cracked and stained. The walls had not been whitewashed for years.

The only place that had a modicum of cleanliness was the small room that acted as their prayer room. Inside, small, brass statuettes of various gods and goddesses were lined up in an orderly way. A lamp was burning though the oil in it was low. From this I.D. deduced that the oil lamp had been burning for at least twenty-four hours.

In the kitchen a fresh loaf of bread, a butter dish and a half-empty bottle of jam were laid on a tray as if the sisters were about to sit down to breakfast. A pot containing about half a litre of milk was standing by the gas stove and a fine layer of cream had formed on the surface. On the gas stove itself tea had been boiled but the gas was off.

In another room, which doubled as a store, lay a heap of hand-knitted garments, unused balls of wool and sundry other things that were part of their business. The room that they used as their bedroom was on a lower floor and here too, the beds were unmade. In the bathroom, there was no shampoo or soaps. There was a single toothbrush that had seen better days but there was no toothpaste. Also missing were towels.

The bodies were taken out of the kitchen and laid out on the drawing room floor. I.D. rang up his superior in the district headquarters and informed him of the double murders. He also examined the bodies minutely and noticed that the diamond rings on the fingers were intact as were the heavy gold necklaces favoured by the sisters. Pappi used to wear gold bangles and they were right there on her wrists. Kamlesh had a gold karah and that too had not been touched. Also intact were their noserings and earrings.

I.D. concluded that whatever be the motive of the murder, robbery was not one of them. This conclusion was based on a rough mental calculation. He estimated that the jewellery on the persons of the two women was worth several lakh and he could not see any reason why the murderer or murderers did not take them.

At the district police headquarters, there was a flurry of activity. A team of detectives was hastily assembled and dispatched to Mansuri along with a dog squad. I.D. decided to inform the local press who took down his statement and flashed the news to their papers nationwide.

Mantri, the chowkidar and the diminutive shopkeeper identified the bodies formally and gave their statements to the visiting detectives. They then went home and Mantri had the odious task of informing an aged aunt over the phone about the sisters' unfortunate demise. She left her house in the valley in the middle of the night for Mansuri and was there early in the morning along with two of her nephews.

That was around the time that Rajni called me and I trudged up the hill wet, chilled to the bone, and reached Cliff Hall. There the police had already placed the bodies in their shrouds, ready for dispatch to the morgue for the mandatory post-mortem. So, I didn't see their faces till the time of cremation later in the evening. But I imagined them.

In my confused state that morning I had not told my houseguest, Mrs Thomas, about the death of the sisters. At that point in time I did not know that Mr Bannerjee too would have had an interest in the matter. While I got engrossed in the results of the post-mortem and the removal of the bodies for cremation in the valley and other such matters, the two of them remained utterly in the dark. It was only at lunchtime, when they asked my staff about my whereabouts, that they learnt that I had gone off to town to attend a funeral. Even then, they didn't know whose.

FORTY-SIX

For a number of reasons, the monsoons are a bad time to die. For one, the process of cremation requires at least three quintals of dry firewood and reducing a body to ashes can take a lot of time. But when the firewood is not dry, as it usually is during the rains, the process can take even longer.

Secondly, all that time waiting for the end can make a man think. Generally, old and sickly people are talked about in muted tones and the usual platitudes are spoken with very heavy doses of hypocrisy, untruth and outright fiction.

But in this case there was much speculation around who and why anyone would have murdered these two rather innocent souls. Since I had been present at the post mortem and had read the doctor's notes on the cause and manner of death, I had different views on the subject. But the handful of mourners assembled there that evening did not know the deceased and so everything was open to rather heavy guesswork. They had come because they were Sikhs and it was part of their religious-social code to be present to give the deceased a sense of identity. Not that the affected cadavers could have cared less.

Up in Mansuri, Mrs Thomas heard the news when she went for her evening stroll. So had Mr Bannerjee. Both were, like all of us who knew the sisters, shocked. That, perhaps, is a mild word. I mean 'shocked'. News like that takes the very breath away because it is not supposed to happen, or so we like to believe. However, it takes time for the message to really sink into the conscious.

The death of a fellow being does that and in most cases, when it is a violent end the general reaction is: 'Thank God! I have been spared.' Like in air crashes.

Sympathy, compassion and a sense of loss seep into the thinking mind in small doses. Those who can cry take their own time to do that. Those who can't, go around with tears on the verge of pouring out, lips trembling in obvious signs of distress, and tongue-tied. But there are professional mourners who will raise shrill cries and tear their clothes to signify pain, loss and grief. But that, we all know, is a bit of a fraudulent act.

In the present case none of this happened. I was told by Mr Bannerjee that Mrs Thomas had tears in her eyes. My eyes had that damp feeling but there were no tears in the real sense. Instead, I was angry. Angry at those who killed the sisters in this most cold-blooded way I could have ever imagined.

After strangling them, the murderers crushed their thoraxes with some kind of tongs. This, the doctor who conducted the post-mortem, told me. He also said that it was the first case of its kind that he had come across in his forty years of practice. This makes it obvious that it was not a crime of passion, he told me. By the way, the women were not raped, he added in parentheses.

Since I.D. and the doctor had ruled out robbery and passion as motives, one could think of only one other reason: the most potent of them all, revenge. The question was, who could have hated them so much as to inflict such a terrible death? One obvious suspect was Pappi's ex-husband.

The police went to see him but he had alibis that could not be doubted. The police also thought he was too effeminate and weak to do the job himself. But he could have hired someone, I argued with I.D. He told me that he had had that checked out too and there was no evidence to suggest that the killers were hired by him. But, he said, it was quite clear that they were professionals.

FORTY-SEVEN

The day after the murder was discovered, Mrs Thomas told me that she would like to go and see Cliff Hall. I told her that it was not such a good idea. For one, there was nothing to see and two, the police had sealed it off. But she insisted and Mr Bannerjee said he would take her as he knew the house.

Soon after breakfast the two of them set off in a taxi. I didn't want to be anywhere near that place.

Instead, I rang up I.D. and asked him if the team of detectives from Dehradun had made any progress. He said not that he knew of. But they had found thick wads of money lying in the folds of their clothes. He thought it was a rather strange way to keep money especially when the women had bank accounts and lockers. Maybe it was black money, I told him.

People did that all the time. Some used sacks to keep their loot, others had special rooms camouflaged as prayer rooms. Some hid their money from the tax people under their mattresses. Nearly everyone in business had some kind of a hiding place for their undeclared money even if it was as innocuous as in the folds of saris and other clothing.

This gave me another idea and I rang up my

American friend Nick, a fellow writer and a thinking man. He lived in the part of town called Little America. Most of the settlers there were American missionaries and educationists. I had told him about the murders and said I had an idea we could discuss over lunch if he could make it. He said he could and we agreed to meet at the Tavern, a restaurant and bar midway between our two houses.

Over some Chinese or what is known as Indo-Chinese food and beer we discussed my theory. The beginning of my premise lay in a simple fact. The sisters, when they stepped out of their house, always carried large tote bags. Most women would have a purse or a shopping bag but these two had these hand-knitted bags with drawstrings. They had become a part of their characters and I think they would have been almost invisible without those bags.

In the bags they would carry a bunch of keys for the shop, the house keys, their knitting, biscuits, tea and coffee, a thick receipt book, small towels to wipe their hands and face, and umbrellas. After concluding the day's business they would also place the cash from the day's earnings in their bags.

No one thought it odd or strange. It was simply part of their persona as much as my caps and hats or someone's walking stick.

I had told I.D. about the tote bags. On the first day of the search of the house, no one had found the bags. They were found the next morning lying under the beds, which was most unusual. The contents mentioned above were intact and so also was some small change.

My theory was that whoever had come to see them that evening had given them a large sum of money as an advance against the sale of the house. (This was before I heard about Khosla's statement to the police.) Since it was after banking hours and the sisters were in a hurry to open their shop on time, they had simply put the money in the tote bags and taken them along with them. It was my theory that someone knew about that transaction and he—or they—came the next morning just as the sisters were sitting down to breakfast.

They rang the doorbell. One of the sisters opened the door because she knew at least one of the men. Then they came in. There was some talk about the proposed sale and suddenly things went sour. Either the sisters refused to sell or demanded more money than they had the previous evening. A scuffle ensued (the post-mortem report mentioned several bruises on the bodies of both the women, as if they were pummelled). The women were overpowered (this supports my theory that there were more than one person in the room at the time of the murder) then choked and strangulated.

Finally, the coup de grace was delivered by crushing their thoraxes with kitchen tongs.

The dead bodies were then dragged into the

kitchen, the door bolted from the outside, the money taken from the tote bags, the bags thrown carelessly under the beds, and the perpetrators made off silently and disappeared into the thick mist.

Nick listened in silence and after pondering over the matter said that it was quite a possible scenario. But then who could the murderers be? Why had the sisters allowed them inside? Or had they forced their way in? There were no signs of forced entry. Why was it necessary to kill them?

We discussed these questions and thought we had found the correct answers. We agreed that at least one of them was a local person, man or woman. That explained the need to silence the sisters forever. That is what we thought. But then life is illogical, as a great man once said.

⸻ ❧ ⸻

FORTY-EIGHT

In his Rishikesh retreat, Shankar the tantric read the news of the double murder. He told his assembly of acolytes that dying led us to moksha, eternal happiness. Two of the ones closest to him said, '*Bhola ki jai.*' Bhola was Shiva, their presiding deity, mentor and guide.

The three of them had returned to the ashram late

in the night that morning and no one knew where they had been. They had sat silently around a little fire and smoked chillum after chillum of quality hash. At first light, one of them had gone to the newspaper-seller near the bus stand and picked up a copy of *Dainik Jagran*.

The guru had expressly asked for that paper because he knew that it would always have a good description of anything that was happening around their area. And Rishikesh was hardly seventy kilometres away from Mansuri.

He read the paper carefully. The report informed him that two women were found murdered in their house. One Inspector Ishwari Dutt led the police party. The paper further said that the police were investigating the matter and a squad of detectives and dogs had been brought up from Dehra, but so far the police had no clues. The hunt was on for the criminals and so on and so forth.

Shankar grunted once and threw the paper to one of the acolytes. The man read through it, smiled and passed it on to his companion. Some other disciples were up by then and they were busy getting the morning fire going. Soon, there was the heavy aroma of parathas being fried and halwa being roasted in pure ghee.

The first serving was made to Shankar, the guru, who after a few incantations to Shiva tucked into his breakfast with dedication. The others did the same and their drug-induced appetites soon made short work of the food. Then they lit their chillums again and silently and contentedly smoked the morning away.

Soon a crowd of people began to collect . They were herded by one of the disciples into orderly lines and made to squat cross-legged in front of Shankar. He then began his morning sermon in a dull, monotonous voice. Each time he paused, his listeners would shout 'Jai Bum Bhola!' It was the same sermon he preached every morning.

After preaching, he retreated into the smaller hut at the back and here he listened and dispensed advice to those who wanted it. He never took a paisa for his advice but as was the custom, the devotees brought offerings of food and fruit. Some of the more satisfied ones would leave wads of money with one of the acolytes to meet the various expenses of the ashram, especially the purchase of marijuana.

FORTY-NINE

Mrs Thomas and Mr Bannerjee visited Cliff Hall though I had advised them against it. They were surprised to see there was no one around and that the front door was unlocked. They pushed the door open and walked into the small anteroom before proceeding to the drawing room.

The gloom had deepened and Mr Bannerjee put on a light to see better. It was a feeble light that fell on the room because the sisters did not believe in having high-wattage bulbs. Those consumed more electricity.

They tiptoed on the dust-covered floor as if they were scared of waking up the dead, and reached the point where the sisters had fallen before being dragged into the kitchen. Mrs Thomas gazed at the spot for some time and then, like a sleepwalker or a blind person, moved to the kitchen with her hands held out in front. Mr Bannerjee followed.

He stood at the door to the kitchen while Mrs Thomas went around touching the pots and pans. In one of the pots the milk had curdled, and a small army of ants was moving up and down the open jam jar. In one corner a huge rat sat chewing on a piece of bread. He didn't seem to be bothered by the two humans looming above him.

Mrs Thomas looked around and Mr Bannerjee saw her eyes were unfocussed and vacant. He realised she was in a trance and that only she knew what she was seeing. Suddenly, a small black dog that the sisters used to call Stray, darted in and began to whimper at Mrs Thomas's feet. She knelt and gently caressed him. The dog calmed down and she looked deep into his eyes.

She must have stared at him for a few minutes, Mr

Bannerjee told me later. Then she abruptly got up and marched out of the door and out into the open. There she stood for a while breathing deeply of the damp mist and then began to walk slowly towards the gate and down the hill to where there taxi was parked. She didn't talk all the way to my house and when she came inside she disappeared into her room. Mr Bannerjee wandered around for a while.

It was around the time I.D. drove over to my house. I was busy in my den writing and when Ratan, my faithful servant, escorted him inside I asked him to bring out the bottle of rum and two glasses. I.D. said he couldn't have a drink as he had to visit his superintendent in Dehra and it wouldn't do to have liquor on his breath. I poured myself a drink and asked him if he had any news of the murderers.

'I questioned Khosla at length and even threatened to put some chilli up his arse if he didn't come out with the truth. But Khosla swore by all the gods that he knew nothing about the murders. He said he had last seen the sisters in the evening when he had visited them with the buyer from Delhi. They had summarily dismissed the two and they had left the house. The Delhi man had even taken out a large envelope with money as a final inducement but the sisters were having none of that,' I.D. reported.

I.D. then said he asked Khosla if it was possible that the man had come back the next morning or late in the night. Khosla told him that even if he had, there was no way the sisters were going to let him inside the house. Besides, he had talked to him in Delhi the next day so there was no question of the man having come and gone.

Khosla was allowed to go because, as I.D. said, he could not get anything out of the man that was relevant to the case. He did, however, manage to get an address for the man in Delhi and planned to go there to follow up his inquiries.

While we were talking Ratan came and told me that Mr Bannerjee would like to see me rather urgently. I told I.D. I had to go and I.D. said he too had an appointment with his superior before he left for Delhi. He left and I went into the drawing room where Mr Bannerjee was waiting for me.

❦

FIFTY

(I have to depend here on what I heard from Mr Bannerjee. There is no reason for him to lie.)

Mrs Thomas reappeared from her room into which she had disappeared, and sat down with Mr Bannerjee. Then she told him what she had seen in Cliff Hall.

According to her, there had been three men. They

had come early in the morning. She described the men as sadhus with long matted hair and beards, ash-covered faces and hands, wooden sandals and dressed in dirty saffron kaftans. One of the sadhus she recognised as the man who had come to see her in her Calcutta flat.

Mr Bannerjee said he assumed it was Shankar.

They sat with the sisters for a while, refused breakfast and said that they had to go ahead with prayer rituals as the time was just right. The sisters had then sat down on the ground and Shankar had lit a chillum. He had passed it around for his acolytes to smoke, although the sisters refused.

The dog Stray sat through the ritual and watched keenly.

The sisters were told to close their eyes and soon, they swooned. Mrs Thomas was not sure what had caused them to faint. Was it the marijuana fumes or something else?

Then Shankar signalled the two men to strangulate them. But as the sisters began to choke they seemed to come back to life and began to thrash around wildly. Then Shankar pummelled them with hard blows to their midriff. That seemed to have succeeded in keeping them quiet and by that time the two men had choked them unconscious.

Then Shankar got up and picked up his *chimta*, the long steel tongs with sharp and pointed ends carried by many sadhus. It is a multi-purpose tool often used by them to give a sort of metallic percussion to their bhajan sessions, to pick up coals to light their chillums and, in an emergency, to fight off an adversary. Used skilfully, it can maim, if not kill a man.

In this case, Shankar went through another tantric ritual. Mrs Thomas saw him crushing the thorax of each sister with his chimta. The acolytes then dragged the bodies to the kitchen, bolted the door from outside and left as silently as they had come.

The only witness to this macabre ritual was the mutt called Stray and it was in his eyes that Mrs Thomas saw the reflection of those horrific killings.

❦

FIFTY-ONE

While I.D. made his way to Delhi, Mr Bannerjee was heading for Rishikesh, to confront Shankar. It is best to recount the events as they unfolded based on both I.D.'s and Mr Bannerjee's accounts.

I.D.'s story:

I reached Delhi late in the evening and reported to the New Friends Colony police station. I explained my mission to the officer-in-charge who then told a young inspector to accompany me to the house of one Mr Sharma, the boss of the man from Delhi. I had his address from Khosla.

At first the sentry at the gate of Sharma's house refused us entry. When we said that we had to ask some questions of Mr Sharma, the man said he would have to check with his boss. He rang up someone in the house and soon, the man who had been to Mansuri and who had gone with Khosla to Cliff Hall, came to the gate.

He asked us what our business was and I told him we were following up inquiries regarding the murders of the two women in Mansuri. He asked us to come in the morning but I was adamant and insisted on talking to him right away or he could come to the police station with us, forcibly, if necessary.

Just then another man appeared from inside the house at the gate. He was an elderly gentleman and politely asked us how he could help. In the faint streetlight I didn't recognise him. But when he moved into the glow cast by the lights on his gate I placed him at once. I had seen the man in Doon Jail where I had been told that he was a film producer but was behind bars for plotting to kill someone in Mansuri.

I sensed I was on the right track because here was a connection with the crime spot. The man invited us inside the house and said his name was Mr P.P. Sharma and he was a film producer. He named some of the films he had made and the actors he had worked with. The younger man, he said, was his secretary.

It was all very impressive but having been in the police for so many years I can smell something fishy from a distance.

He also told me that the secretary had visited Mansuri recently to talk about a property that was reportedly on the market. But the deal had not matured as yet and he was hopeful that it would soon.

When I heard this I told him that the sellers in question, two elderly ladies, were murdered within hours of his secretary's visit, Mr Sharma expressed alarm and said he was indeed very sorry to hear that. But he rather forcefully explained that neither his secretary nor he had anything to do with it.

I then cleverly put it to him that I knew about his time in Doon Jail. It was also in connection with an attempted murder in Mansuri. And jumping the facts a bit, I put it to him that there was a connection between those who lived in Cliff Hall and him.

The man turned white in the face and, from a confident and arrogant old man, he suddenly turned into a fumbling, bumbling old fellow. He fell on his knees and said that he had nothing to do with the murder of the sisters. He grasped my leg and said he would swear on anything that he was innocent.

I now knew that I had a suspect. Actually, two of them. I told them that they were under arrest and would have to accompany me for further interrogation to Mansuri. Their two servants, who were hovering in the background, caught my eye and I remembered them from my visit to Doon Jail.

Mr Sharma then begged me to let him go and said he would be willing to pay anything. I stuck to my guns. I told him rather sternly to get packed and get set to leave immediately. He begged for some more time. He said he would leave first thing in the morning because it was not good for his health to travel during the night. I said nothing doing and after roundly abusing him, bundled him and his secretary into the taxi I had brought from Mansuri.

The inspector at the local police station took the two servants into custody and said he would hold them for me till I could send another party to bring them to Mansuri.

We left for Mansuri the same night and from a phone booth on the way I rang up my deputy and told him to send another party down to Delhi to pick up the other two suspects.

(I.D.'s language is often crude, full of expletives and policemanlike, and may have upset some readers, so I have taken the liberty to make it sound more proper.)

—◦◦◦—

FIFTY-TWO

Mr Bannerjee's story:

I reached Shankar's ashram in Rishikesh just as the evening aarti was getting over and the sun was setting behind the hills in the west. I was warmly welcomed by the tantric but I refused his offers of hospitality and in a rather cold voice told him that I needed to talk to him privately. He asked me what was wrong with talking in his ashram and I said it wouldn't do. I took him to a hotel on the banks of the Ganga where I booked a room.

Shankar told me the strangest story I have ever heard in my life. And there are many that I've heard as Moni Baba, and in my wanderings as an ascetic. When I first asked him why he had murdered the two sisters he was taken aback.

'How do you know?' he had asked.

'Mrs Thomas told me,' I had told him.

The mention of Mrs Thomas's name immediately made him think, and he began his recital of the story that lasted for the better part of the night. But I will try and make it short and to the point because there are a lot of details that are not worth going into. Nor are they pertinent to what happened.

He said his association with the sisters was about a year old. A man called Khosla, who claimed to be a journalist from Mansuri, had introduced them to him. They would often visit him at his ashram when he was in Rishikesh and talk about their problems. Many a time they had tearfully explained to him that their lives were empty and they had contemplated suicide. What worried them the most was that they had no one to leave their property and wealth to.

'I tried to persuade them against the idea of suicide as I said it would not help them attain moksha and freedom from their karma. They would be reborn again and again and live their lives as insects, dogs, cats and all other kind of lowly creatures. They said that was better than the life they had led so far and would have to keep living if they did not jump into the Ganga or consume poison,' Shankar said.

'One day they told me that they were determined to end their lives and had come to my ashram to hand over a will in which they had stated that their property and wealth would belong to me after their death. They said that they had had their assets valued and the property alone was worth about four crore. Then there was personal jewellery and cash.

'I explained to them that all that meant nothing to me. I had no use for their property or their money. But they kept on insisting. I told them to go home and think about the matter.

'That was about three months ago. Two weeks

back they came again and said that they had made up their minds. I told them there was a tantric ritual that I knew which would end their mortal lives and release their soul from the eternal cycle of birth and rebirth. It was better than committing suicide, which was a sin.

'I suggested this ritual to them because I had also been told by this man called Khosla that one P.P. Sharma from Delhi wanted to buy their property. He had asked me to persuade them to sell it to him. I didn't like this man Khosla and I remembered what you had told me about the lives of these women and the way they were treated at the hands of Babuji.

'It seemed like a good idea to find out more of this man called P.P. Sharma. After all, why was he interested in only *their* property and not any other? My people in Delhi found out all about him and it turned out that this P.P. Sharma had recently been released from Doon Jail. He was none other than the crook called Babuji and the same man who had brought so much shame to my old friend and guru bhai Sudip and to you.

'What a better way to take revenge than by sending him back to jail as a suspect for the murder of the two women! No one would miss the women as they had no one in the world except themselves. After considerable thought I described to the women what the ritual was about, and they agreed to undergo it.

'When they told me that there had been a visitor to

their house accompanied by Khosla, and he had shown great interest in the purchase of their house, I knew the time was right.

'My acolytes and I left early next morning for Mansuri. It was raining heavily and no one was about to have seen us entering their house. The rest, you know.'

As you will well understand, I was more than dumbfounded by what Shankar told me. I didn't know what to do after listening to his side of the story. But before leaving him I asked him about the will.

'Oh, that piece of paper? I tore it up and threw it in the Ganga. It should be food for the fish by now,' he had said, laughing.

FIFTY-THREE

A little knowledge is a dangerous thing, one wise man has said, and the law is an ass, another wise man has observed. And the upholders and implementers of the law, that is, the police, exemplify both these. I.D. was one of the bigger examples.

He was in a good mood after having arrested P.P. Sharma, his secretary and the two servants. He had produced them before the chief judicial magistrate and, after explaining their background and previous convictions, asked that they remain longer in police remand.

That was a misnomer, if there ever was one. Police routinely use that time to torture and interrogate their suspects and eventually force them to sign confessions. It saved them a lot of legwork, collection of forensic evidence, unreliable eye-witnesses and other routine paper work.

In my house, the debate between Mr Bannerjee, Mrs Thomas and myself was about the question of handing over the real murderers to the police. Mr Bannerjee and I were in favour of letting Sharma suffer some more time in jail. Another jail sentence would surely kill the man, we reasoned.

Mrs Thomas was against the idea. She said she would rather see the tantric Shankar and his acolytes hang. Whatever we may have had to say was overruled by her stubborn defence of her psychic powers that had established that Shankar and his accomplices were the murderers. We talked of euthanasia and such alternatives but she dismissed all that as against morality, decency, integrity and the will of God. Besides, she said that Shankar had admitted to the crime.

Is doing someone a favour a crime? we asked. She would not be moved.

After much discussion we decided to let I.D. into the secret and let him decide. To this Mrs Thomas agreed.

When I.D. came over to my house armed with a bottle of rum to celebrate his triumph I told him we would have to invite my houseguests to his little party. He said the more there were, the merrier.

Mrs Thomas waited till she thought it was time to tell I.D. what she knew and what Mr Bannerjee had confirmed. By that time I.D. was three sheets to the wind, and had recounted the adventure of the arrests with some embellishments. He said he was going to see that the old man was hanged. The last time, he had got away with a simple imprisonment, because it was only an attempted murder. But this time he had him dead to rights and while he had no forensic evidence he was going make the bastard sign a confessional statement.

The old lady made a sign for him to stop and said she had something to tell him. In rather simple words she told him that he was wrong, had the wrong men in custody, while the real murderers were sitting around scot-free. That sobered up I.D. to some extent and he asked her how she knew.

Mr Bannerjee entered the conversation and said he had gone to meet Shankar the tantric in Rishikesh. This was because Mrs Thomas had seen the murderers in a trance and recognised Shankar. In Rishikesh, the tantric admitted to the murder and had also told him that he did it because the sisters wanted to die. I think I.D. would have fallen off his chair if I had not reached out and held him up. He was so shocked and speechless that he sat there for quite a while, his jaw hanging loose, his shoulders in a slump and his body language telling all that he had lost his moment in the sun.

After restoring his wits with a large shot of rum he cleared his throat and said that he had motive and that Sharma had been preparing to take his revenge for a long time. He had told him so, he said.

I agreed with him but explained that Shankar was sure to get away in a court of law because he had no motive, nothing to gain and Mrs Thomas's instincts would be totally lost on the judge. She would most probably be laughed out of court. So he should go ahead and crucify Sharma.

By now I.D. was having second thoughts about the whole case. What he thought was a waterproof case against Sharma was lacking in several details. First, there were no eye-witnesses. Then, no fingerprints. No traces of the attackers. The more he thought about it the more he realised that a simple confession made in police custody was these days not considered evidence in a court of law.

The same applied to Shankar. Even if he arrested the tantric, where would he get material witnesses? He would look foolish in a courtroom full of unbelievers if he put Mrs Thomas on the stand. Mr Bannerjee would get the courtesy given to old men and fools.

The more he thought about it the more solace he

found in drink. And as time went by he fell asleep with his head on the table. Mr Bannerjee and Mrs Thomas had left earlier and it was left to me to have him taken out to his jeep and sent back to the police station. I called his driver and bodyguard and between the two of them they carried him off like an injured football player.

⸺◦◦◦⸺

FIFTY-FOUR

The sisters' death wish made for some interesting conversation between Nick and me when we met next. He felt that the tantric should have been handed over to the police. But when I explained that the man was nowhere to be found and had disappeared into the wilderness, he saw the pointlessness and futility of trying to chase a sadhu who did not want to be caught. He could vanish among the millions of his kind spread all over the country. And anyway, the police were not equipped to take on such a massive search.

He thought there was some poetic justice in Sharma being behind bars for the second time. But I had my doubts about that. I had seen and read about how many criminal trials had gone sour because either the witnesses turned hostile or simply went missing.

The record of the courts in these matters of conviction was pathetically dismal. Chances were that Sharma would be set free.

Coming back to I.D. He went through the motions of getting the case prosecuted. In his heart of hearts he knew that Sharma would get away. He had the money to get himself the best defence, and the public prosecutor was severely handicapped because the police had provided him with no solid evidence to nail the man.

I.D. felt cheated. On the day of his retirement he came to see me. In a voice full of loss he said he had made many mistakes in his life as a policeman. But the biggest was when he refused the money offered to him by Sharma to let him go free.

'What difference would it have made to the victims?' were his parting words.